The
Wedding Gift

Jesse L. Dunn

ADDED UPON PUBLISHING
USA

ISBN 978-0-9740319-4-1
Library of Congress Control Number 2012909579

To my wife, my best friend

Whose gift of light brings joy to the world

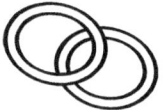

Prologue

The attic was a mess. For years she promised herself she would get around to taking care of it, but there was always something more important to get done. Some people liked sorting through endless piles of dusty memories stored away for some future replay. Corinne Johnson Whitmore was not one of them. She preferred to have something else to do. Anything else. Live life today, on its own terms—that was what she believed. And so the attic was pretty much the same as it was when Edward died nine years ago.

Today, however, she found herself squeezing through the little door into the dark room. She fumbled for a moment, finally finding a small turn switch. The light from a single bare bulb in the left center of the space provided little improvement, but it would do. She could see boxes of every shape and variety stacked and strewn about.

"Garage sale fugitives," she mumbled to herself. She put her hands on her hips, sighed the resigned sigh of the condemned and dug into her task.

The whole idea of entering the sleeping world of the dusty attic was to find a suitable gift for her great-granddaughter's wedding. Corinne was fiercely independent—always had been— and she wanted to give the couple something nice. She supposed she could go to the J.S. Williams department store and review the bridal registry. But she was practical and understood that she lived on a fixed income. "A fixed income," she groused. "I wish they'd fix mine." Besides, at her age, she figured she ought to be passing along some heirlooms to spare the grandkids squabbling over her stuff when she died. She had a lot of stuff. "Not that any of it's valuable," she told herself, "except for sentimental value, of course."

Corinne took her hands off her hips, rolled up her sleeves and pulled open the cardboard box nearest to her. At 88 years of age, she was alert and alive and feeling as strong as ever since her husband Edward left her a widow. She didn't plan on joining him any time soon. She enjoyed herself immensely these days. She had made the delicious discovery that old people—*really* old people like her—could pretty much get away with whatever they wanted. If she was sometimes a bit eccentric or even bizarre, family and friends quickly forgave her, attributing it to her advancing years. She playfully milked that discovery for all it was worth—never in a manipulative or malicious way—but with a deliberate fun that tweaked the prideful and self-righteous among her descendants. It was amusing to watch them squirm when she bluntly spoke her mind. It was fun to see them react to her with wide-eyed caution. The serious "uppity" ones among them were thus kept deliciously off-balance as she returned to being "sweet ol' Grandma" again.

Edward and Corinne had seven children, four girls and three boys. Their youngest, Tommy, was killed as a young teen in an automobile accident. The others had grown to marry and make families of their own. She now had 24 grandchildren and 23 great-grandchildren. "That's one thing we Whitmores know how to do right," she once observed. "We know how to make babies!" The one getting married tomorrow was Michelle, her oldest grandson's oldest daughter.

Michelle was one of Corinne's favorites. Her parents were Jeb and Ellie. Jeb was the oldest son of Edward Jr., Corinne's oldest boy. His wife Ellie was from the Allred family—good people, descended from the original pioneer stock that helped establish the small mountain town of White Lake.

Jeb and Ellie, like their parents and grandparents before, had settled down in town, choosing its more simple life over higher paying jobs in the big city.

They were the only ones from Corinne's family who did that. The others were scattered in places like Seattle and Los Angeles and Philadelphia and other spots all over the country, and even in other parts of the world. One of her grandsons had his family over in Sweden. It was impossible to keep track of them all these days.

Except for the family who stayed, of course. Jeb was an assistant principal over at the White Lake County High School now. Ellie sold Avon to her friends. Every now and then, Corinne bought shampoo from her that smelled like fruit.

Now their daughter was getting married. Corinne could scarcely believe how fast little Michelle had grown up.

Michelle and her brother Jeffrey visited often when they were younger. They called her "Grammo." Michelle's child tongue could not pronounce "Grandma" and when it came out "Grammo" the name stuck. She loved it. Michelle worked as a receptionist down at Heath Parker's insurance office. It was good work and Corinne was proud of her.

"What in the world should I give them?" she wondered aloud. That first box had some of Edward's old papers in it, nothing of use to her there in solving her dilemma. She dragged it off the stack out of the way and attacked the next box.

So great granddaughter Michelle was marrying the Jensen boy. He was Tom and Jennifer Jensen's oldest son. "What's was his name?" Her brow furrowed as she tried to think of it. "Mark. Mark Jensen, that's it."

Corinne first met the boy at church. He and Michelle walked around arm in arm and when they sat in the pew, you couldn't squeeze a butter knife between them. "Now that's budding love," Corinne thought with a smile.

She wasn't surprised a few months later to hear they were getting hitched. "He's a nice boy. Good family. His mother was a

Hatch. Makes a good living, something to do with computers. He's kind of quiet though," she decided.

She sorted through several more boxes. She started a pile of a few things that might work. "Trinkets and junk," she thought, not yet satisfied. "Michelle is so talented musically. I wish I had kept one of Ed's violins for her."

The three violins had ended up in her second daughter Cathy's family. Cathy was musical like her father and it seemed the obvious thing to do at the time, but Corinne now regretted giving them away. Cathy's arthritis prevented her from playing them anymore, although she kept one of her father's instruments for sentimental reasons. The other two were passed along to Cathy's daughters Karen and Diane. They didn't really play and didn't really care. Corinne supposed Edward's violins were gathering dust in some closet now. "It's a shame," Corinne thought, "Michelle would love one of them." She didn't know if Mark Jensen was musical or not. "Young people don't get enough culture," she mused. In her day, good music was one of the true pleasures all could share. "It's television that's done us in. That and that loud screeching racket that passes for popular music with the kids these days."

There was some jewelry, but "she's not really that kind of girl," and some old glass bowls that Corinne thought she received from her mother. "Those might be nice," she thought as she placed them carefully to the side.

As Corinne fished through another box, her fingers rubbed the grainy cover of a small leather book. Carefully she removed it from among the other contents and gently brushed thick dust off the outside. The rich smell of cowhide brought an avalanche of colorful memories cascading powerfully from her past. "Oh, my," she whispered. "I haven't seen this in many a year. I'd forgotten all about it!"

She ceased her wedding gift pilgrimage for the moment and descended the stairs with her new found treasure. She sat down slowly in her favorite chair and put on her reading glasses, adjusting them to sit halfway along the bridge of her nose. Her hands gnarled with age, she tenderly undid the ribbon binding around the outside of the little journal. Eagerly she looked at the first page, a page she herself had penned more than 69 years earlier.

Suddenly, Corinne was swept away in memory to days long ago when she was a fresh bride. It was a wonderful winter, a wonderful way to start a wonderful new year and new life.

Chapter One

January 17

Today was the best day of my life! I've dreamed about this day for years, and now my dream has come true. Ed Whitmore and I united our love in sacred vows of marriage this afternoon at 2:00 p.m. He is the kindest, most handsome, simply wonderful man I know. And that smile! Of all the marriages made throughout history, ours is destined to be the best because we love each other so much. And, as everyone knows, love conquers all. And we will.

We wanted it to be a simple wedding, which made it simply heavenly. The reception was very nice, too. I didn't know so many wanted to wish us well! There are so many wedding gifts that it will take a month just to write the thank you letters! That will be a happy task when I can finally get to it.

We'll leave for our honeymoon in the morning. We're driving down to Colorado in Ed's Chevrolet. We'll be back in two weeks to start our new life together. I can hardly stand the wait!

Corinne Whitmore worked on the last of the Thank You letters. The reception was wonderful and the gifts plentiful. The honeymoon had been exciting. They were nearly ready to settle into a life of their own. Just a few more little house decorating ideas and then she would be ready to live happily ever after. After completing the gift acknowledgements, of course. She looked at the little card in front of her and pondered what to write. "Ed. Ed, darling, how do you think I should respond to old Mrs. Williams' gift?"

Edward put down his fiddle, which he had been playing softly while his new bride wrote. She gazed glowingly at him. She loved to hear him play. He was so talented and handsome. He placed the bow across his lap. "What do you mean, my sweet? Why can't you just send her a thank you letter like all the rest?"

"She didn't give us anything like all the rest."

"Yes, well, she is a bit odd now, isn't she? Very rich, but, how do they say… eccentric. I suppose it's because she's getting along in years, her mind getting muddled what with her being shut up in that huge house and all."

"She must be terribly lonely. You know, she and her husband were inseparable until he died eleven years ago. People say they were always like newlyweds, even after being married so long. " She looked at Edward to see if the last point had registered, but he was picking around on the fiddle already thinking of the next tune. Young Corinne fingered the card Sarah Williams had presented to them at their reception just before the honeymoon. It was written neatly and attached to a small box with a white ribbon.

"Listen to what she wrote, Ed," as she read out loud. It said, in its entirety,

> *Come over to the house when you get back. Bring the box.*
> *Best wishes, Sarah Williams*

Corinne held up the contents for Ed to see. The box contained an obviously used pair of nail nippers and a nail file. "Perhaps tomorrow we should call on Mrs. Williams. Ed, what do you think?"

Edward stood and put his fiddle back in its case. "I still think anyone who gives a newly married couple used items of a personal nature is batty." He regretted the comment as soon as it left his mouth. He froze as Corrine's glare bored in on him. It was the first time that his wife gave him "The Look."

Now Edward was a new husband. He was inexperienced and so there was no way he could have anticipated it. He froze in his seat when he was caught by it. "The Look," of course, is that piercing glare of displeasure eventually familiar to all married men throughout the ages. Edward would be a much older man before he figured out "The Look." But today he was completely naïve and pitifully innocent—a rank amateur and rookie in his very first game going up against a natural professional.

Squirming uncomfortably, Edward sought quickly to get back into his bride's good graces. "You are right. She probably is very lonely. I'm afraid tomorrow, though, I have that insurance meeting on the new motor inn cabins we're building on Highway 30."

He looked hopefully at his bride to see if he was on the right track. Her frown told him that he wasn't.

"Of course, I want to go visit her with you, if you'd like me to. Could we think about Sunday afternoon? We could take some ice cream and visit properly with her."

"The Look" faded and Corinne's face seemed to brighten at this last suggestion. Edward was pleased at his apparently successful recovery. He had survived his first clumsy blunder. All was well again. Relieved, he walked over to the fireplace, grabbed the poker and tried to stimulate a little more heat into the small room.

"Yes," Corinne said, "let's make a visit on Sunday." She neatly stacked the Thank You cards and stood up from the table. She walked over to her husband, grabbed his right arm to swing him around, and planted a big kiss on his lips.

CB

Sunday afternoon was cold and clear. Edward and Corinne walked tentatively up the narrow sidewalk to Sarah Williams' front door. The house was large and well kept, despite its obvious age.

All was still and quiet—no sign of activity. Edward looked at Corinne, then shifted the pint carton of chocolate ice cream he brought as a gift to his left arm and swung the knocker.

No one came. He shifted his weight from one foot to the other then knocked again. Silence. Just as Edward and Corinne started to turn and leave, the large door cracked open. "Who is it?" Sarah's voice sounded distant and frail.

"It's Edward and Corinne Whitmore, Mrs. Williams. We've come to thank you for your wedding gift." Corinne clasped her handbag tightly as she spoke, not knowing what to expect.

The door opened widely. "Well, come on in! Hurry up, hurry up! You're letting cold air inside."

Ed and Corinne stepped quickly into the entryway.

"You should have let me know you were coming," Mrs. Williams scolded. "I would have tidied up a bit. You'll just have to excuse the mess." She said this as if it were terribly obvious the place was in shambles, but Corinne thought everything was neat as a pin.

The house was one of the oldest in the valley. James Williams had built it over the years after he and Sarah moved in and helped settle the area. Together they turned a large plot of land in the business district from sagebrush and sand into the first general mercantile the region had. They worked hard. Along the way, he was elected to represent the region in the state legislature. She became famous for her business acumen and foresight, building something of a retail empire in the little town.

They had six children, five sons and their youngest, Maggie. Corinne didn't know anything about the boys. She vaguely remembered her mother mentioning something about two of them dying in some sort of fire when they were teenagers. But Maggie she did know about. Maggie Williams was the jewel of the valley, a beauty pageant queen and a top-notch musician. She had married and moved away though. Somewhere on the West coast. Yes, the Williams family was a legend in these parts. Everyone admired their happy family and wonderful marriage. In time, they accumulated assets—mostly land—which they turned into solid wealth. Some believed they were the richest and most famous couple in the region.

The interior of the Williams' home reflected some of the finer things in life. The rich luster of wooden furniture (mostly cherry, Corinne observed) was polished to a bright sheen which glowed, even in the dim light. Upholstery on the cushions was exotic and elaborate. The high ceilings and huge chandeliers and floor length draperies and intricate wood mouldings and beautifully woven room-sized rugs and original large paintings and the massive fireplace and …

Corinne felt herself spinning around and around admiring the luxury and beauty of Mrs. Williams' home. There was a serene, peaceful feeling about the place, like everything was in order and always would be no matter what turmoil might occur in the world outside. This is what a home should be, Corinne thought to herself.

She snapped out of her reverie at the sound of Mrs. Williams' voice. "What is that bucket tucked under your armpits, young man?"

Edward quickly pulled the carton into a more suitable position. "It's … I thought … that is … we thought, perhaps, you might enjoy some ice cream." He held it out to her.

"Don't like ice cream," she mumbled. "Hurts my teeth. I still have my own teeth, you know."

Edward stammered, completely flustered at the blunt response to a noble gesture. "I'm sorry. We … I … just thought … we didn't know."

Mrs. Williams grinned, obviously enjoying Edward's discomfort. "Well, tell me one thing. Is it chocolate?"

Edward and Corinne both nodded.

"Well, why didn't you say so? Chocolate makes all the difference—only flavor worth a nickel when it comes to ice cream.

Here, let me put it in the ice box and we'll dish some up later." Edward gratefully handed the carton to her and he and Corinne breathed a sigh of relief. "Now you two go into the sitting room and I'll be with you in just a minute."

The couple hesitantly took seats on a small sofa, the love seat. Corrine sat on the edge, hands clasped to her knees.

"Would you like something to drink?" she called from the other room.

Corinne glanced at Ed who shook his head slightly. "No, thank you," Corinne called back. "Thank you for asking."

At length, Mrs. Williams returned and sat in a large overstuffed recliner just to their right. They sat silently at attention as she eyed first one and then the other. After what seemed like a full minute of this soundless staring, her gaze at length rested upon Edward. She pointed a frail, bony finger at him.

"So, Mr. Whitmore, you are now a married man."

"Yes, ma'am." Her abrupt manner caught him by surprise. "Then tell me, what are you going to do about it?"

Corinne looked at Edward and saw him squirm in his seat. She choked back a giggle that started welling inside. Puzzled he said, "I beg your pardon, ma'am?"

She chuckled. Then Corinne chuckled. Edward smiled weakly, not yet quite alert to the meaning of the moment. "Young man," Sarah Williams began, her voice now noticeably more tender, "Mr. Williams and I were married for 61 years before he passed away. Most people looked at us and thought we had a fairy tale life together."

"Yes! Your marriage is a legend in town! All the girls still talk about it. What was it like to be married to the richest man in this part of the state?" Corinne swooned.

Mrs. Williams shifted her gaze to young Corinne and paused. "Well, young lady, he wasn't rich when I married him." Corinne quickly understood her meaning, and sat back in her seat, nodding.

She turned back to Edward and continued. "When James asked my father for my hand in marriage, my father wanted to know what his intentions were. It's not easy for a father to turn over a precious jewel like his daughter to someone so young and terribly inexperienced, you know. Do you understand what I'm saying?"

Edward nodded his head as if he did.

"Well, of course you don't. How could you possibly know? You're just at the beginning and you haven't any idea what is ahead of you." Sarah again fixed her gaze on the new husband who shifted uncomfortably in his seat. "Why did you marry Mrs. Whitmore?"

"Mrs. Whitmore?" Edward muttered, picturing his mother. "I married Corinne ... oh, yes! Mrs. Whitmore! Of course! Mrs. Whitmore!" The idea had not really registered with him before. His wife now bore his name. That had to mean something.

Sarah smiled patiently. "Well, Mr. Whitmore?"

"I married her because I love her." He knew as soon as he said it that it sounded trite and wholly inadequate. "And because I want to spend the rest of my life with her," he added quickly, vainly searching for substance. Who was this old lady to be quizzing him like this?

"Yes. That is wonderful. Just about the same thing James said to my father," Sarah mused.

"Well, I do," Edward emphasized, a little defensively. "Corinne means everything to me." He reached over and clutched her hand in his, looked briefly into her eyes, then confidently at Sarah Williams. Corinne blushed and leaned a little closer to her new husband.

"I'm glad that you do, Mr. Whitmore. Mind if I give you a little advice?"

Edward wasn't sure what he was getting into, but relaxed his erect posture slightly and nodded.

"Of course you mind. But please indulge an old lady who was married a long time and believes, foolishly or not, that she has learned a thing or two about men and women and marriage."

"Mrs. Williams, everyone in town talks about what a happy couple you and James were." Corinne said with obvious admiration. "When the women are talking together of how marriages should be, yours is always one they bring up."

Sarah chuckled. "My dear, that is simply because I've outlived anybody who knows anything about it."

"No, Mrs. Williams, I doubt that. If Edward and I can be like you and Mr. Williams, I couldn't ask for anything more," Corinne enthused. "And we are happy. Edward is a wonderful man." She squeezed his hand as she said it. He gave a gentle squeeze back.

"I'm sure he is, dear," the old woman said, her eyes softening as she looked at Corrine. She paused a moment, gazing into the distance, as if seeking for an invisible horizon. "Well, it is true James and I were happy. I consider myself greatly blessed to have had such a wonderful life with him. We did it together. It didn't just happen, though. We made a wagonload of mistakes before we could grow it into something good and noble and sweet for the both of us. We were still working at it, still learning when Mr. Williams passed away."

Corinne's eyes widened in mild surprise.

The old woman smiled again. "You are just at the beginning, my dear. I know you think things are perfect now. I remember how I felt about James when we were first married. Keep those feelings as long as you can. You, too, Mr. Whitmore. Let that feeling of having married the perfect partner be both your foundation and vision on those days when you disappoint each other."

Edward and Corinne both nodded—she fully optimistic that nothing either of them could do would ever disturb the love they felt for each other, and he trying to hide the fact that it was all a bit beyond his comprehension right now.

"How will you support your young bride, Mr. Whitmore?" Sarah suddenly asked.

Edward let go of Corinne's hand, sat up and moved forward to the edge of his seat. Finally, the old woman was getting to the core of the matter. He was prepared for this kind of "advice." With passion and enthusiasm he began. "I work for Tom Perkins right now. I'm a salesman."

"At Perkins Insurance and Real Estate? Fine man. James and I have done business with him for years," Sarah noted.

Edward took encouragement from her words. "I have dreams and plans, Mrs. Williams. The valley has many natural attractions with the cave and the hot springs and canyons. Skiing is becoming big in other parts of the country and can be here, too. Times are tough for a lot of folks in the area and everywhere right now, but that won't last forever. Just think what it would do for the town and people here if we became a place people wanted to come and visit. I plan to be in the middle of that when it happens. I saw what it could be like when Corinne and I were in Colorado for our honeymoon."

Corinne gave him a little look, not realizing until now that their perfect honeymoon had also been a business trip for her husband. Edward didn't notice and continued. He became more animated and his voice more excited as he spoke.

"I know we can do the same thing here. In fact, we're partners in the building of the new motor inn cabins just north of town on Highway 30."

Sarah Williams nodded. "Ah, yes. I heard about that project. Trying to buy a piece of the Nate ranch for that, if I remember right. I believe it's probably one of the few loans the bank is willing to make these days. Selling that piece of land might keep the Nates in their home, though."

"Yes, and that's just the beginning."

"Must keep you very busy, Mr. Whitmore."

"Yes, ma'am, it does. Hard work is the way to succeed and I'm determined that Corinne and our family will enjoy the best."

"That's nice. How do you feel about it, dear?" The old woman shifted her attention to Corinne.

"Ed is wonderful. I know he'll succeed at whatever he decides to do. He works hard right now while we're just starting out. A lot of hours. But even if he doesn't become rich, I'm sure he'll make me happy, Mrs. Williams."

"Do you hear what she is saying, young man?"

"Yes, ma'am, I do. It's a great thing to have a wife who supports you."

"Mr. Whitmore, she is saying she'll support you, but there is more you should understand right from the start." Now it was Sarah's turn to lean forward, her voice raising a notch in intensity. "You see, marriage is not just a sideline for a woman. It is her whole life. That is her natural desire. Relationships are more important than riches to her."

Edward glanced at his new bride. She wore a transcendent smile as she gazed at Sarah Williams. Edward looked back at Mrs. Williams, who wore a similar smile. He quietly, soberly nodded his head as if he understood.

"This is important. In fact, I want you to write down what I'm about to say so you don't forget it."

"I won't forget," Edward said, once more a little defensively.

"Well, of course you will. Don't argue, just write. Then you can pull it out every so often and remind yourself of what an old woman told you one night. That way, as you figure things out in your marriage over the years, you'll have something to look at and say, 'Oh, yes! This is what that shriveled-up ancient prune was getting at.' And even though I'll be gone by then, if I am permitted to look over your shoulder, I'll be saying, 'I told you so!' Here," Sarah pulled a tablet out of the little lamp desk at the right of her chair. "You can use this."

It was Corinne, not Edward, who reached automatically for the pad of lined paper. Sarah chuckled. "You want to get it right for him, don't you dear?"

"Just making sure it's legible," Corinne grinned. "Ed's marvelous, but he will not win any penmanship contests any day soon."

"Well, that's all right. Of course you want to help. Well, if the truth be told, James' writing wasn't much to look at either. Kind of like chicken scratching—little marks all over the page..." Sarah chuckled.

She then grew serious. "We took a long time together to figure out some of the things I'm going to tell you. Wish we'd known them right from the start. Of course, once I've said them, some of these things will seem obvious to you."

Sarah began to talk. Corinne began to write. Edward listened as best he could. The two women might as well have been from another planet as they discussed things he had never in his simple life even thought of. With a mixture of awe and resignation, he accepted there were things he would have to learn that were as new to him as walking was to a baby.

Edward lost track of the precise time, but Sarah Williams must have continued for at least another hour and a half, maybe two hours. He felt like he was in the presence of a master and he couldn't keep up. He did not interrupt. His head was spinning. He felt like a little boy again on the first day of school.

Corinne, too, worked quietly, writing as rapidly as she could to catch the main ideas Sarah Williams shared with them. Her words flowed like a deep river. Occasionally the two would exchange comments. Sometimes they would laugh together. At these moments, Edward wondered what he had missed.

Then she was finished. "Oh, look at the time. I've gone on way too long. I'm afraid I've bored you."

Yes, a little, Edward thought.

"No, not at all," Corinne protested. "I just feel like a tiny teacup trying to hold a gallon's worth of wisdom. This is wonderful! How can we ever thank you?" Edward silently nodded in agreement.

"Well, for one thing, dear, come back tomorrow with the gift I gave you." Corinne promised to come back at one the next afternoon with the box. Edward would be working, but Sarah was most interested in visiting with Corinne anyway. "The second thing you can do is help me eat this ice cream I have in the ice box."

☙

It was dark outside when Edward and Corinne finally walked the short distance back to their new home. "That was something, wasn't it?" Edward asked.

"Yes it was something," Corinne agreed. "She was like a dam with a giant reservoir built up. We show up and she opens the gates ..."

"Why us?" Edward wondered.

"I don't know. Maybe because we live so close. Maybe because her children are so far away. I don't know."

"I wonder if her kids got the same lecture."

"It wasn't a lecture, Ed."

"You know what I mean."

"She's complicated and fascinating," Corinne mused. "I think there's a lot we can't understand about what she told us tonight. I wrote down as much as I could, but I still missed so much."

"I'm sure you got much more of it than I could have. Thanks for rescuing me in there." Edward squeezed her hand in appreciation.

Corinne smiled and squeezed back as they reached the porch and front door. They walked inside, turned on the lights and hung up their coats. "This was a wonderful evening, Ed. Thank you."

"I didn't do anything."

"Yes. Yes you did. You went with me when you didn't have to."

"I love you."

"I love you, too. I'm happy we're married."

Later, as Edward and Corinne prepared to go to bed, Ed asked, "I think I'd like to stay up just a bit longer and think over some things. Where are those notes you took at Mrs. Williams' house?"

"I put them on the kitchen table, honey."

"I think I'll stay up and just look them over, if you don't mind."

"Of course I don't mind. Hope you can read my writing. Come to bed soon. Good night."

"I love you, Corinne. Good night."

⚃

Edward sat down at the kitchen table, sipping hot cocoa. He set his cup down and pulled out the sheaf of notes his wife made earlier.

February 1-- Notes from visit to Sarah Williams ...

Edward smiled to himself. He loved the way Corinne wrote things out, like she was a schoolgirl doing a report. It was a cute and endearing thing.

Of course, he thought, Corinne always did get "A's" in English class. In fact, as he thought about it, she got "A's" in practically everything. Smart girl. And pretty, too. He thought himself very, very lucky. She could have had any boy in town or in the valley, for that matter. Edward knew some who were wealthier and some who might be thought of as better looking. Somehow she chose him, an unrefined young man who outwardly showed very little promise. His smile broadened. He picked up the cup and took another sip. He leaned back in his chair and moved the papers to his lap.

Edward instantly saw that Corinne had organized and numbered the notes on the page. Her talent amazed him. He flipped through quickly to see how many points she had gleaned from Sarah Williams. It looked like there were ten. He studied the first.

1. Men and women are totally different creatures… Well now there's an astonishing insight, Edward thought a little sarcastically. *God wants us to live as males and females.*

2. Belief in God is the bedrock of successful marriage.

Edward recalled that Sarah Williams referred to God a lot during the evening. He admired her obvious faith. He knew Corrine had a strong belief, too, so it didn't surprise him that she captured it in her notes. Edward didn't disbelieve—he grew up accepting God's existence, along with the religious traditions of his family. But to him God was an abstract; he was more interested in practical things like earning a living and making his mark on the world. He guessed that what Mrs. Williams meant was that a husband and wife should have the same spiritual values. He was confident he and Corrine were on the same page with that…

3. Women were selected by God to be mothers. Men were selected by God to be fathers.

Edward sat up a little in the kitchen chair. Another reference to God. He remembered that when Mrs. Williams mentioned that God selected him to be a father earlier this evening, it hit him like a mule kick in the chest. It was a sobering thing to be selected for anything, but picked by God for an office—the job of father—was a bit overwhelming to him at the moment.

4. God wants us to be happy. His plan of happiness is a gift from him. The centerpiece of his plan is marriage. Marriage is where families are made. Family is to be a bit of heaven on earth. "When we walked through the doors into our home, we tried to act as if we were passing through the gates of heaven."

Mrs. Williams' words reminded Edward of something his mother told him once: "Home can be a heaven on earth."

5. *The differences between a man and a woman are supposed to fit together to make a complete whole. Oneness in marriage doesn't mean sameness—it means wholeness.*

That was something Edward could understand easily. Men were to be men and women were to be women. Together they accomplished far more than they could individually.

6. *There are evil forces in the world that seek to confuse roles and disrupt marriage the way it is intended to be. They try to make men and women enemies. There is no such thing as a "battle between the sexes," only selfishness and confusion.*

Edward paused his reading to ponder this one a while. Before they were married, he and Corinne had occasionally discussed how things were different today than they used to be. It used to be that evil lurked in quiet, dark corners. Today it seemed to parade arrogantly down main highways of society, shamelessly flaunting itself. Magazines, books, music and even radio made jokes about men and women and marriage. They made a big thing out of this supposed war between men and women, as if there were some genetic or natural force that made them quarrel. He and Corinne didn't think it had to be that way when they were married. It was reassuring to hear someone like Sarah Williams say the same thing.

7. *To be happy, men and women will not envy the unique roles of one another.*

8. *We women have the capacity to bear children. Many women naturally have special gifts of nurturing, compassion, gentleness, tenderness and spiritual sensitivity. Her influence is the refining and civilizing power in the family and society.*

Edward turned the page sideways to read a little note with a star beside it: *Sarah is so good at this and I really want to be!* A tiny smile curled at the corners of his mouth. Corrine was so serious about this marriage stuff… He quickly moved to his new wife's next note.

9. The man's nature is to preside, provide and protect. Preside means to assume responsibility for. His role demands sacrifice of self to preserve his family. I've seen this in Ed already!

Edward swallowed hard as he read the last sentence. Was he really as willing and as self-sacrificing as his bride believed him to be? What would—or wouldn't—he do for her? Swim the proverbial shark-infested waters for her? Crawl to the ends of the earth to bring her what she needed from him? Fight off hordes of invading barbarians to save her? Be a father to their children? Be kind to her? Speak soft words to her? Love her?

The thought briefly crossed his mind that he had walked in to something he was not well prepared for. He was in over his head, and now he knew it.

Number ten was underlined.

10. Practice the seven secrets …. What are these???? She will tell us another time.* CW

Edward leaned forward and set his cup down. He smiled that his wife signed off her note taking with her new married initials. Then he sat back in the hard, high-back chair. He yawned and leaned forward to push away from the table. "Seven 'secrets?' I wonder what that's supposed to mean," he thought briefly. But it was very late, way past time for bed.

As he stood to go join his wife in their bedroom, he noticed another note scribbled vertically in the margin. He craned his neck to the side so he could see to read it.

* Mrs. Williams, tomorrow, 1:00 p.m. Bring nail nippers.

Chapter Two

Love not shared is no love at all.

Corinne knocked at Sarah Williams' front door precisely at one the next afternoon. She carried the box with the nail nippers and file, as requested. She also remembered to put a small notebook and pencil in her purse. "Just in case," she reasoned.

"Come on in, dear, I've been expecting you." Corinne was startled by Mrs. Williams' voice. She hadn't heard the door open. She walked quickly inside. As she took off her hat and coat and gloves, she once again admired the richness and luxury of the interior of the Williams mansion. She noticed a violin and clarinet hanging in a glass case on the wall at the foot of the massive stairway. Were those there last night? She didn't know and couldn't remember. It looked a bit odd to her now, something out of place in a home otherwise so exquisitely decorated.

"I'm happy you decided to come back," the old woman said as she led the way into the sitting room. "After you and your young man left last evening, I was afraid I sounded too much like a senile, old fool."

"No, no, not at all," Corinne protested. "Do you know Edward stayed up last night just to look at my notes of what you said? We talked about it this morning."

"You did? Oh, dear me!" Sarah remarked. "What did I say?"

Corinne was confused. "Well, you know, about the home being a bit of heaven on earth, and how men and women are different and that's the way it should be and …"

Mrs. Williams was smiling, the soft glow of aged wisdom in her face. Corinne relaxed just a little. With a nod of the head, Sarah said, "You brought the box, I see. That's nice."

"Yes," Corinne quickly said, holding it out to her.

"Open it, dear, and come over to me." Mrs. Williams slowly turned and eased herself into a large, overstuffed chair, propping her frail, right foot on the ample ottoman in front of her.

Corinne moved haltingly toward the old woman, unsure of herself.

"There, now, that's a good girl. Help me off with my sock, would you please?"

Corinne glanced at the elevated foot in front of her. The red woolen bootie was worn and faded, no doubt painstakingly hand-knit many years ago. The sanitized smell of old skin suddenly nauseated her. She's not feeling well today, Corinne concluded. Or maybe she doesn't quite remember who I am.

"Oh, go ahead, dear. Nothing's going to bite you!"

Gingerly, Corinne reached out and pinched the end of the slipper with three fingers. She carefully tugged. It slid off with surprising ease. Gnarled toes curled delicately like dry twigs from the pale, shriveled small mass that greeted her. Long, yellowed nails covered the tiny tips.

"Please go on," the old woman coaxed. "Would you be kind enough to trim my nails for me? It is a little hard for me to manage at my age."

She doesn't actually want *me* to cut *her* toenails, does she, Corinne wondered in amazement. Reluctantly, she knelt beside Mrs. Williams, opened the lid of the box, and withdrew the nail nippers. So that was it. Sarah Williams needed someone to help her out and, being the clever woman she was, gave a wedding gift to Corinne to get her to do the job. Well, this would be the last time, that's for sure. She swallowed hard, grabbed the frail foot and started on the big toe.

"Ow!" Mrs. Williams howled. "What do you think you're doing? Are you trying to torture me to death, child?"

Corinne stood quickly, apologizing. "I'm sorry, I'm sorry. I was just trying to ... well, I was just ... Oh, Mrs. Williams, I'm so sorry!" She stuffed the nippers back into the velvet resting place in the box.

Sarah Williams reached forward and massaged her toe. "Gently, dear. You must be careful. Begin at one edge, you see, and move methodically along. The blades are good and sharp, so you don't have to cut away at it. Trim, don't cut."

Corinne was not sure this was a lesson she quite appreciated. She looked for her purse, thinking to leave. Unfortunately, she had placed it on the small table at the left hand of Mrs. Williams. It would be too awkward to retrieve it. Besides, Mrs. Williams had hung her coat in the closet and that would have to be rescued as well. Not to mention that it just would not be socially acceptable to attack the big toe of one of the oldest and revered women in the valley and then run away leaving her to suffer. No, she was trapped.

"Relax, child. Don't be frightened. Now try it again. Gently this time."

Corinne hesitated. She saw no alternative but to do as the old woman requested. Carefully she trimmed along the top of the toe. Mrs. Williams sat forward slightly, peering to scrutinize the work of her young guest. Corinne proceeded slowly, grimacing and tense, fully expecting to hear another shriek of pain or to draw blood or maybe to accidentally amputate the digit she now operated upon. Fortunately she succeeded in completing the task without further calamity. One toe trimmed. She concentrated on the next nail atop the long neighbor adjacent to the big toe.

"This is a very kind thing, my dear. Thank you."

Corinne remained focused on completing her task. "My pleasure," she lied and continued in silence.

"It's only in the act of giving that we can love," the old woman said at length.

Corinne was nearly finished with one foot, but stopped her work long enough to hear what surely would be sage advice.

"Yes," Mrs. Williams continued. "Without the actions to back it up, it's a bunch of puffed up fluffery. Take you, for instance."

"What about me?"

"I know you are a loving child because here you are doing something you absolutely do not wish to do."

Corinne was caught. This was one smart old lady.

"Now, now... I know. It's all right. But even though you didn't want to do it, you are still here. Why?"

Corinne opened her mouth to answer, but the old woman did not give her the chance to speak.

"I'll tell you why. It's because you have the heart of love. You're able to give, even when you don't want to."

"Thank you, Mrs. Williams. I'm trying to do what's right." About this, Corinne was sincere.

"I know, my dear. Just remember the first of the seven secrets: *love not shared is no love at all.*"

Ↄ

He loved her from the first time he saw her at the community dance. They called them "Barn Dances," even though it had been years since one was actually held in a barn. Now they were in the large assembly room at the town center in Marshville.

She was dressed in her blue and white calico dress that fit just perfectly. With her soft locks of brown hair curled gently on her shoulders and bright, laughing eyes setting his soul afire when they met his, Sarah Daly was irresistible.

Jimmy Williams was no dancer. He would rather be the fiddler in the band. He actually did play a bit, but he kept that news to himself, for he was too shy to actually let others hear his music. Dancing, on the other hand—well, he might as well have been swimming upstream in the dead of winter on the frozen White Creek. It just wasn't any use. His feet never quite matched the music.

Everyone knew he couldn't dance. Earlier in the evening he had approached Miss Linda Murphy, who was no belle of the ball herself. She was sitting with two or three of her girl friends over on the west side. "May I have this dance?" he politely asked.

"Sure," she replied, "I don't want it." She then stood and walked away with her giggling friends close behind.

That's what it was like to be Jimmy Williams at a community dance.

Add that to the fact that he was a gangly looking fellow and it didn't give him much hope with the beautiful Sarah Daly. He also noted that she did not lack for male companionship. Seemed like every guy in the place was lined up for a dance with the elegant Miss Daly. Boy, she sure was pretty.

Despite the odds against him, he couldn't help himself. He just had to try. Screwing up his courage, he turned around and shuffled forward. To his horror, he stepped on the foot of the very young lady he sought. He stood speechless, humiliated beyond words.

Sarah winced, but smiled graciously and ignored her pain. "You're Jimmy Williams, aren't you? I've heard about you. Let me introduce myself. I'm Sarah Daly." She put out her right hand and he took it.

Hi, I'm...uh... Jimmy. Jimmy Williams." Too late, he realized that she already knew that.

"I know they call you Jimmy, but is it all right if I call you James? I think James sounds more distinguished, don't you, and I think it fits you better. James Williams. Yes, very nice."

That is how Jimmy Williams came to be called James. He was amazed. First of all, that she knew who he was. Second, he hadn't said one word to this beautiful being and already she had carried on a bubbling conversation all by herself.

"Um, I… uh… that is…" James swallowed hard, terribly self-conscious. "Would you care to dance?" he finally stammered.

Miraculously, she said yes.

James later considered it the most considerate thing anyone had ever done for him in his entire life up to that point. He felt completely at ease with this sparkling, bright woman. He didn't have to worry about his dancing or being something he wasn't. They began courting and in time it was clear to both of them that they made a good couple. They had little when it came to money or things, but that didn't matter much back then. Nobody did, to speak of. What they had was a belief and commitment to make things work.

Sarah's father was dead set against it. "He's just a bag of sawdust," he frowned. "That scarecrow will never amount to much, you mark my words." But like protective fathers before and after, he underestimated his daughter and James Williams.

Six months later they got married.

On their wedding day, James told Sarah he would do anything in the world for her.

"Anything?" Sarah asked with sweet innocence.

"Anything!" James naively confirmed.

She believed him. She believed he loved her and really *would* do anything in the world for her. Of course, James was thinking more along the lines of simple things like taming a ferocious bear or moving a mountain.

About a month into the marriage, remembering his kind promise, Sarah asked James to trim her toenails. Her father used to do that for her mother who was bent with painful arthritis. All of the children watched their father perform this gentle, loving service once every four or five weeks.

So when her own husband offered to do anything in the world for her, Sarah asked him to do the same thing. It would carry on a loving tradition. She imagined a sweet scene as her new husband, down on one knee, gallantly took the foot of his gorgeous bride. Like a knight of old heroically drawing his sword, he would whip out his nail nippers, blades gleaming in golden sunlight, and with deft agility trim the noble nails of the one he loved. Then with a tender kiss on the top of the foot, he would tell her eloquently of his undying commitment to her, how he was honored to have performed this deed for her, and how she could still count on him to do anything in the world for her.

James did not quite share his wife's romantic vision about the nail-trimming chore. This wasn't bear-taming, mountain-moving stuff.

"It is not man's work," he responded quite matter-of-factly. "I think you are perfectly capable of cutting your own nails."

Sarah was stunned. Until that moment she perceived James to be the most perfect husband. Like anyone beginning life together, they didn't start out where they ended up.

Sarah was hurt and responded by doing what came naturally to her at that young age. She threw a tantrum. A "hissy fit" as James called them. Sarah let him know in no uncertain terms that her feelings were hurt. She said some angry words. He was humiliated. She ended up crying and he ended up walking out of the house and riding his horse to his thinking spot.

Sarah Williams' in later years wistfully reminisced about James' thinking spot.

"We had this little house—a shack really—with a little hill to the west," she recalled. "James would ride to the other side of that hill to a clump of rocks where he'd sit and sort things out. It was his private place back then, until we moved into the valley here. I wasn't supposed to know about it. He'd forget, though, and every once in a while he'd talk about it. It took a few years, but I finally learned that a man needs to have his thinking spot, a place to go to where he can just catch up to himself. I didn't know it back then, though. I thought when he rode out that day that he didn't love me anymore and was just trying to get away from me."

The fact was, they were both awfully pig-headed. He wasn't gone very long. He came back a little while later, but he didn't say anything. Sarah figured he was just trying to act like nothing had happened.

"He must've been lying when he said he'd do anything for me," she thought. "He won't trim my toenails and now he won't talk to me! He obviously doesn't care about me at all! What kind of man am I hitched to?"

Sarah then went through a phase of blaming herself. "Maybe I am too demanding. Maybe there is something wrong with me and my feet are too disgusting to him."

For his part, James just went back to doing his normal chores and working on his plans for the business he wanted to get going.

They lived in Marshville, which was a nice place, but was real small in those days. James and Sarah both wanted someday to live in a place where they could get a general store going, where there were enough people and enough activity to succeed.

A few years later they did move up north to the large town of White Lake, but first they had to get back on the right track with each other.

Sarah tried to talk to James about it a few times over the next few months, but he wouldn't have anything to do with it. He would just clam up, go silent and clench his jaw. One day Sarah got up the courage to ask point blank why he told her he would do anything in the world for her, yet wouldn't trim her toenails. He looked at her silently. Without a word he walked out the front door, mounted his horse and took off to his thinking spot.

The icy period lasted until December of that year. In his way, James tried his best to make it up to his new wife. It's just that his way to patch things up was completely different than anything that made sense to her. "After all," Sarah thought, "if a woman's new husband was not sharing his love with her, what was she to do?"

"Of course, I would just sit down with him and communicate about it," she answered herself. "Communication is the key to relationships."

That was a woman's natural way. But to James, that kind of thing didn't mean love at all. All along, he thought he *was* showing Sarah that he cared. He really thought that, after a few weeks anyway, everything was fine with her and between them. He figured he was making it all up to her by all his hard work, which he said was for her. He worked long and hard that first year. He was determined to be a good provider. He farmed a bit—got a good crop, too. He hunted some when they needed the meat. He did a little ranching, dealing in livestock. A lot of folks were into that down Marshville way.

Most importantly, he got his wife set up with a little candy shop in the center of town. It was a dream of hers to have a candy shop. He worked a miracle to get it arranged.

Some miracles take time to develop and take time to see how big they really are. That's how it was with Sarah's candy shop. Over time, Sarah's candies became famous in nearly every town west of the Rockies. The rich chocolate sweets melted like the food of gods in the mouth. But it was small and struggling that first year. Yes, James had worked a miracle to get it all arranged for her. Now it would take business smarts and real effort to keep it going.

Sarah truly appreciated all his hard work. And she could *think* that it meant he loved her. She just didn't *feel* it. She wondered if something was wrong with her, but in any case there was just something missing and she wasn't happy about it. They weren't connecting, not really sharing like she thought folks in a good marriage should. Without sharing, there wasn't real love, or so she thought.

Her mother (as most mothers do) had advice for her daughter. "Take what he has to give. He's working hard, doing good things, but darling you're twisting it to make it look like he is just doing them to further himself or so he'll look good in the eyes of his family or your neighbors. Seems like you won't let him share. Is that, maybe, because you want to hear only certain things you think means 'love'?"

Her mother was wise, but Sarah's hurt clouded her mind until December.

It was their first Christmas together. She so wanted it to be special. They went together to the other side of the hill near their little cottage. Above the rocks that were his thinking spot, James cut the most perfect tree. They took it home and decorated it with balls and candles and treats Sarah made. It was beautiful. The smell of pine and the soft glow of candlelight and gifts under the tree brought a wonderful feeling to them both. There was a softer, more peaceful spirit in their home.

"I don't know what to get for James," she told her parents.

He'd been hinting at a few things for the barn—some leather and tools, things like that, you know. Those things were practical. That's the way James thought all the time—practical. She knew whatever he had wrapped up under the tree for her would be something practical. She guessed it would be something they needed for the kitchen.

"That is all right," Sarah thought. "I'm sure he expects me to be happy and grateful for a gift like that. And I surely would be. But I want my gift to him to be something meaningful, something that shares my love with him. But what?"

The days went by and as Christmas approached, she still hadn't decided. It turned out to be a busy time of year for the little candy shop, and Sarah worked from early morning, cooking until late at night. Time and energy were running out.

December 24th was especially long and busy. Her dream was that every child in Marshville would have a sweet treat that Christmas. She knew that some might get no other gift at all. She was determined. From morning to night, she cooked and wrapped and sorted. James made deliveries to the homes and ranches all around. Some drop-offs he made anonymously, where there could be no way for a father to pay for the sweets for the children. It was just understood they were from Santa Claus.

Of course, those same folks came back to the store when times were better, buying a few extra candies for a special occasion. And they soon told others, too. "Best advertising I ever did!" Sarah modestly said later, "So as a business deal, it all worked out in the end." It was typical of Sarah Williams' generation to humbly hide their obvious generosity.

While James was out that Christmas Eve on one of the last deliveries, Sarah's father came into the shop carrying his old violin. Frank Daly was a great musician and played at all the dances in the town.

"Give this as your present to James," he told his daughter.

"No, Papa, that is your finest fiddle! Besides, what in the world would James do with that?"

He knew very well Sarah didn't have anything else for her husband. He also knew that here on Christmas Eve it was too late now to try and get anything else.

"I have another," he reminded his daughter. "James is family now. That makes him like a son and any son of mine has to keep up the family fiddling tradition!" Frank Daly's eyes twinkled and then he chuckled with that "pleased-with-myself" laugh that made it hard for Sarah to refuse.

He was insistent. "Besides," Sarah spoke as she tried to convince herself, "a fiddle would be a pleasant diversion for James."

Most importantly, it wasn't too "practical," and that's what mattered to her that first Christmas. So, she swallowed her pride.

She took the fiddle, thanked her father, and finally closed the candy shop for the night. She went home, arriving before James and wrapped up the gift, disguising the shape as best she could. Then she placed it under the tree in as inconspicuous a spot as she could find.

They had a nice little program together that Christmas Eve. Just James and Sarah, their own little family in their own little home. Sarah still remembered decades later the warm feelings of love and peace that night as they sang carols and read in the Bible about the Lord's birth. They made it a tradition every Christmas they had together after that.

The next morning they woke up early. James built a fire in the stone fireplace to warm up the small living room. They had their morning prayer. Then they exchanged gifts.

James opened Sarah's present first and he was thrilled. "I thought you would give me something practical, like that leather awl I've been needing. But this is perfect! Oh, goodness, my own fiddle! You know, your Daddy and I get together every once in a while and play some tunes. Thank you, thank you so much dear. This is the best Christmas present I've ever had!" Then he gave her the biggest and best kiss she'd had in a long time.

Sarah felt ashamed. She had been married to the fellow going on a full year and she didn't even know he played the fiddle! She was so happy that he was happy. And she was suddenly thankful for a wise father who, it was clear to her now, really did know everything after all. She realized that he sure made his daughter look good in the eyes of her new husband that year.

"Now it's your turn," James said to Sarah. He handed her a little package, a box shape, about eight inches long by four inches wide by two inches high.

"About the right size for a new salt and pepper shaker set for the kitchen," Sarah thought. She suddenly felt a little depressed that she was going to get salt and pepper shakers while he got a fiddle.

Sarah slowly undid the carefully wrapped bundle. It was a small, finely polished cherry wood box, approximately eight inches long and four inches wide. On top was a plain small card on which her husband had scrawled, "I'll do it. Love, James."

Gently she opened the golden clasp and pushed open the hinged top and looked inside. Sarah laughed and then she cried. She simply couldn't believe what this wonderful, splendid man of hers had done. "Oh, James!" She began to weep with joy. "It's the best gift I've ever received!"

Resting inside the little box on plush velvet lining was a splendid set of fine nail nippers.

ɢ

Monday, February 4.

I visited Mrs. Sarah Williams today. She asked me to cut her toenails with the nail nippers she gave us for a wedding gift. I didn't want to at first. Then she told me where they came from and how they were a special gift of love shared by her husband the first Christmas they had together. It proved to Sarah that James really would do anything in the world for her. I wish Edward could have been there. I told him the story at dinner tonight. It was good.

Love not shared is no love at all.

Chapter Three

Forgive. Let it go. Leave it alone.

The Whitmores stayed very busy the next few weeks. Edward spent long hours at work preparing for the land purchase negotiations and poring over the design plans for the motor inn cabins on Highway 30. It meant coming home late each night and left him so dog-tired he had little energy left for anything except a simple dinner and dropping into bed. Too soon, it was up again at dawn and back to the office for more drawings and contracts and documents.

Then there were his insurance policies to sell. He was supposed to contact the townspeople to discuss their life insurance needs and set up appointments every day. Sometimes that meant meeting in the evenings. It was how he got started in business and it was how he made most of his money. The commissions were good. But even that part of his job lately was taking a back seat to the big development project.

It was a grueling routine that he couldn't keep up forever, but he knew in the long run it would pay off handsomely. He would be a wealthy man by valley standards in a relatively short time. Then, he reasoned, he would make it up to Corinne and spend more time with her enjoying their lives. They could even begin a family. Meanwhile, he was sure she understood and supported him. Besides, it was all for her.

Meanwhile, Corinne kept herself busy with housework. She wanted to be a fabulous wife and so she did what she had been taught by her mother and grandmother and their mothers a thousand generations back. Her every act was designed to please her new husband. The thought of making him happy made her happy. She decorated their little dwelling so Ed would have a comfortable place to come home to. She cheerfully worked tedious hours knitting and sewing and making pretty little things. She began collecting items that would come in handy for future children, like blankets and cute stuffed toys. A big part of each day was spent preparing food and cleaning up, cooking meals she hoped Ed would really like. As much as she could find the time, she read books and papers and magazine articles of all kinds so that she might be interesting when talking with Ed and their circle of friends. She purposed to make friends with other wives whose husbands were going places, who would someday be influential.

Whenever Ed noticed her hair, or a new picture hung in the hallway, or her great cooking, she was greatly pleased. When he didn't say anything, she silently went back to work, trying a new recipe or a different hairstyle or redecorating, to make it all the perfect nest. Every day, she made herself pretty to greet him when he came home. Lately, though, he too often didn't come home until very late at night.

The development project was at a critical stage. And Edward really believed that she understood. She was a good woman and a wonderful wife. He loved her.

At first, Corinne *did* try to understand. She knew it was important to Ed to do well. She felt she was completely willing to sacrifice her needs for a short while so that he could get his career going. By all accounts, Ed was making good progress. Maybe it would only be a few days longer. And she believed him when he promised to make it up to her.

But leaving early in the morning and returning home late at night soon became the routine, not an exception. A week of it and

Corinne began to feel a little neglected. Two weeks and she started to feel lonely. It was well into the fourth week in a row that she felt angry and resentful. There was no need for it. The project was dragging on. There were more important things in life and this didn't have to take all of his time and attention. It seemed to Corinne that Edward was falling in love again, this time with his work, leaving her on the sideline. She saw excitement in Ed's eyes as the thrill of seeing his dreams become a possibility. She also saw that he didn't count all the costs. Maybe he didn't even know what they all were. She could tell him. She wanted to support him, but he seemed to love this new mistress more than he loved her.

The big problem was figuring out what she could actually do about it. She would have a better idea if Ed was falling for someone else. At least she could confront the other woman. But how could she face up to this lover, who had no mind or soul or body, yet consumed her husband more thoroughly each passing day? Occasionally, she tried to talk with Ed about it. But she could never quite say it right and her attempts to connect with him on the subject always failed.

Edward's replies were always to the point. It annoyed Corinne that he was so mechanically logical about it. With cold, unfeeling reason he started from the premise that he was actually being a good husband, which is all he ever really wanted to be. Now that they were three months into their marriage, the best way for him to be a good husband, he believed, was to provide for her needs and build for their future family. He noted that the best way to provide was to work hard and make sacrifices now while he was young, to get ahead while he could, so that they could benefit from it later. He would secure the necessities and even a few of the good things in life for her in this manner. If she would just expand her view a little and look down the road, she surely could see the common sense in all of it. It was a plan that would work.

He knew it was hard for just a little while, but she was tough—that was one thing that attracted him to her in the first place—and it would all be worth it in the end. Or maybe she was just being a little bit selfish and ungrateful. Didn't she know it wasn't easy for him to get up every day and work such long hours so that one day she could have the life she dreamed of?

Only, it wasn't the life she dreamed of.

Ed's cold logic exasperated Corinne. She got irritated at the "poor me—selfish you" messages he indulged in. When he said she was selfish, they argued angrily. That made them both feel worse. Why couldn't Ed figure it out? He was a smart, ambitious guy. He could certainly see that providing "things" was only a part of providing for her and their family. Surely he knew that providing love and tenderness and understanding was the only capital that created any wealth with her.

Not that she didn't want nice things. Money, security, a good house, a successful husband, respect—she wouldn't mind any of that. It was sweet of Ed that he tried so hard to provide them for her. Of course, there were no guarantees, even with her husband's great efforts. Didn't he know that his success at work made little difference to her? It was not *his* success she dreamed of. It was *their* success she wanted. The life she dreamed of had to do with love and happiness and joy in each other and their family.

Corinne talked to her mother about it.

"What's the problem?" her mother kept asking.

She was a widow who lived on the other side of town. Corinne saw her about once a week, often doing her grocery shopping for her, and helping with chores around her home like laundry. Her younger brother Clay was still at home. He was sixteen and big and strong, but a lazy boy at heart who didn't help his mother much. He was more interested in carousing with his friends, who were the sort who could never win the approval of his sister and certainly not his mother. If only their father was still around. He died when Corinne was eleven and Clay just six. They'd pretty much been on their own since then.

"What's the problem?" her mother wanted to know. "You have a man who loves you and provides for you. You're not starving, you know."

Yes, Corinne knew.

"You have a lot more than I ever had, especially when your father passed away and I was left with you two still so young," her mother reminded. Do you remember how tough things got? No, I suppose you were too young to understand." They were a charity case for a couple of years until her mother was lucky enough to get that job down at the Woolworth's store. It had been humiliating to her to have to do that. "I wish you could remember all that, young lady, because I can't for the life of me figure out why a daughter of mine would complain about a man like Ed who wants to give her good things in life." She shook her head in embellished astonishment.

"But what about love?" Corinne wanted to know.

"Love is shown in many ways," her mother said. "What you need is to be grateful and let Ed get on with his work and put away this foolish, romantic notion about what marriage is supposed to be like. Love? Why, my dear, any fool can see that Ed loves you about as much as any man could. You should learn to understand and accept it."

And that was that.

Corinne tried to resign herself to her mother's advice. She was quiet about her feelings for almost a whole week. But the loneliness was a dull ache in her heart and the misery a dense fog shrouding her soul.

One day, after more than a month of Ed's work routine, Corinne sat in her front room. The cooking and cleaning were done. There was nothing left to redecorate. It was just quiet and lonely. She gazed past frilly curtains out the window. It was sunny and warm. Too warm for early March. It was like the earth was pregnant with Spring, not due until mid-April, and today had gone into early labor. False alarm, Corinne knew. Another day or two and it would most likely snow. She closed her eyes and let mild fingers of sun caress her cheeks and forehead. She loved the light.

It was love that she yearned for. Not money, not things, not even security like her mother talked about. She couldn't quite get her mind to say what her heart screamed at her. She knew it when she saw it. Ed loved her like she needed to be loved before they were married and for two months after their wedding day. This obsession he had now to provide for her wasn't love, at least not to her. She knew a lot of people who had plenty of money and no love in their marriages. Maybe it was too hard to have both. If you couldn't have both, she concluded, she'd take the love, because love makes you richer in the long run.

Then she remembered of Sarah and James Williams. They had money. And love. And happiness. I should go over and visit, Corinne thought. Maybe she needs her toenails trimmed.

☙

Sarah Williams was slow in coming to the front door.

"Good afternoon, Mrs. Williams!" Corinne greeted cheerfully. "How are you today?" The old woman was wrapped tightly in a large shawl, looking pitiful and frail.

"Who is it? Who's there?" She squinted into the white sunlight from the musty darkness of her entryway. "What do you want?"

"It's me, Mrs. Williams. It's Corinne Whitmore."

"Who?"

"Corinne Whitmore."

"Corinne? Whitmore?"

Corinne thought that the woman stooped over in the doorway looked especially old and vulnerable today. "Yes, Mrs. Williams. It's me. I've come to do your nails, if you'd like me to."

40

Sarah Williams brightened. "Oh, yes! Of course, my dear, come on in. I'm sorry. I've been expecting you."

Corinne knew she wasn't really expecting her, but stepped quickly through the door into the entryway.

"You'll have to excuse the mess, my dear. I've not been up to taking care of everything I should just lately."

The house was dark, dimly lit by random rays of sun poking through cracks where tall drapes met large windows. A glare off the glass case by the stairway showed layers of dust. The violin and clarinet Corinne first noticed more than a month before were still on shrine-like display, their mystery still intact.

The old woman shuffled very slowly toward the sitting room. "Here, take my arm," Corinne offered. She led Mrs. Williams to the large chair with the footstool. "Are you feeling all right?"

"Oh, better than any other woman my age in this town, I suppose."

"Mrs. Williams, you are the *only* woman your age in this town," Corinne laughed.

"See what I mean?" she joked. "Considering the alternative, I feel wonderful! But you're not going to ask me to dance a jig, are you?"

Corinne chuckled again. "Would you mind—I mean, would you like me to open the draperies and let some light in for you? It's a beautiful day today."

"Is it? Oh, would you, please? Some days I don't have the strength to draw them. Thank you, very much, dear."

Corinne quickly hopped up. As if by magic, the room came to life when she opened the massive curtains, allowing the warm light to come flooding in. Sarah squinted, then tipped her head back and drew a deep breath, the burst of sun purifying the room's stale air.

"Oh, that's lovely. Heavenly. I do so love the light, don't you? Thank you."

"You're welcome." Corinne crossed the room and kneeled by the stool on which Mrs. Williams propped her feet. "Would you like me to trim your nails?" she asked sincerely. "I brought the nippers with me."

Sarah smiled. "Yes. I would like that."

Corinne went to work. Unlike her last attempt more than six weeks ago, this time she proceeded confidently, with a sense of genuine service. She removed pink woolen booties from the feet of Sarah Williams, and then carefully and methodically trimmed each yellowed nail.

"This is nice of you, my dear," Sarah said. "Did I tell you those nippers were a gift from my James on our very first Christmas together?"

"Yes…" Corinne started to answer.

Sarah told the story again as Corinne trimmed. "Always after that, if he was available, he'd trim my toenails for me," she concluded. "It was something my daddy did for my mother. It was a good tradition. It was James' special, secret way to tell me he loved me."

Corinne enjoyed the image, though she doubted Ed would even find the time these days to discuss it, much less actually do something like that in their family. "That is so nice, Mrs. Williams! Everyone knows how you and your husband just loved each other so!"

To smooth any rough or uneven edges, Corinne had thought to bring along the small nail file. She made a few quick easy fixes on lesser toes, then concentrated on the crooked big toe of the right foot, which needed far more attention. Mrs. Williams was smiling, relaxed.

"How do you and your husband like being married, now that you've been at it for…" Sarah's brow furrowed as she tried to remember. "How long has it been?"

"Three months."

"Three months?"

"Yes. It's hard to believe, but it's been three months already."

"And how do you like it?"

The question caught Corinne by surprise. She hesitated, unsure of how much to open up. "Well, Ed's working very hard these days. He's anxious to make a good living for us, you know."

Sarah nodded wisely, still smiling. "James was that way early in our marriage, too. That's a good thing, dear. You wouldn't want him hanging around the house all day messing it up and driving you crazy!" she winked.

"I only wish he paid more attention to me," Corinne replied.

"Well, don't be too put off, dear. It's the way men are set up. It's like they can't help it. If they love you, they want to provide and take care of you."

Corinne was sullenly silent, still struggling with how much to share.

"In every marriage there comes that time when you have to start settling in," Sarah explained. "It's kind of a let down from the excitement of your honeymoon or of setting up a new home as a couple. But it's the nitty-gritty time of getting down to the daily business and routine of living life with each other."

"I suppose so." Suddenly, Corinne could hold back no longer. "I can't explain it, but to tell the truth, I'm disappointed," she began. "It seems Ed doesn't want to be with me anymore. He's so insensitive to what I really need him to provide. I'm … I'm … well, frustrated and lonely and … I'm angry! How can he do this to me? And blame me for being selfish? How can he do this to us?" She let out a gasp of air, surprised at her own release of anger.

"I understand, dear. I'm sure you have a reason for feeling this way."

Corinne then shared her story, how Ed spent more and more hours at his work, how he had this "plan" but forgot to include her, how he wanted to be rich but left her alone. "I don't care if we're rich. I just want to be together—you know, to be happy."

"Of course you do, dear."

"It's like his drive for success in business, to be wealthy, is more important to him than anything else in the world."

"Wealth is an alluring and powerful seductress."

"Well, you and Mr. Williams were rich and still happy, weren't you?" Corinne pressed earnestly.

"In time, I guess it looked that way to others, yes. We were happy and I guess you could say compared to some we were rich. It took a long time, though. We weren't in any hurry." Then, thoughtfully, Sarah added, "We finally figured out the two really aren't related all that closely."

Corinne nodded in eager agreement. "I don't think they are either. Ed won't see it, though. I just don't know if I can forgive him for pushing me aside like this. And after only three months!"

"Of course you can, dear. And you will. Just give it a little time. You'll be all right."

"I don't know about that," Corinne said, a little defiantly. "I feel betrayed. He's the one who needs to change things."

"Swallow your pride, child, or you'll choke to death on it."

Corinne said nothing and took a deep breath, trying to calm the waters of the sea of emotion boiling inside her.

"Corinne, come and sit down here with me awhile. Let me tell you a little story that not many know about James and me. Would you do that, dear?"

Corinne nodded, "I'd like that. She helped Mrs. Williams slip her booties back on and slid over to the sofa. She sat on the edge of the plush cushion and listened intently as Sarah Williams began.

⁐

One day, a little more than a year after James and Sarah married, she excitedly greeted him with the news that they were to become parents.

"When?" he asked.

"Sometime in October. Isn't it exciting?"

"Yes. Yes, of course," he stammered. The poor man's eyes became wide with amazement. "How ...? I mean what ...? That is, how do you know?"

"Let's just say woman's intuition," Sarah chuckled. "It will be fine, dear. Just think! A family of our own. I wonder if it's a boy or a girl." The light of happy dreams flashed in her sparkling eyes.

James quietly nodded. "Um, yes. Well, that's wonderful, darling." He tried to sound enthusiastic as he reached out to give his wife a dutiful hug.

Everything progressed fine through the summer, although Sarah became increasingly uncomfortable as she grew. Dr. Simmons would come by every once in a while to look in on her. He was a pleasant fellow with a rotund red face and a belly to match. This physical fact, coupled with his jovial disposition, the good doctor reminded Sarah of Santa Claus. She wasn't sure he quite understood this business of having a baby, though he had delivered hundreds throughout the valley over the years. It all seemed a big joke to him. But Sarah didn't mind too much. He was the only working doctor around.

One evening James dragged through the door after a long day's work. Sarah cheerfully greeted him, "Hello, dear! I'm so glad you're home. I've got some exciting news!"

"Oh?" James replied warily. He hoped her news would be inexpensive and go easy on the family budget.

"Yes! Dr. Simmons came for his visit today."

"Well, what do you know? What did he have to say?"

Sarah bit her lower lip, tentative about continuing. "First, he predicts we'll be parents about the third week in October."

James nodded, quickly calculating in his head what that meant in terms of the costs of getting ready.

Anxiety creased Sarah's forehead. "He also said I was a little bit large for this stage of things. He thinks we might have twins."

The news slapped James like a whipping pine branch. He didn't know what to say. He numbly took Sarah in his arms and held her a little while without speaking. Could he do it? *Two* babies? The thought numbed him. While he made his living working on his father's ranch, plans were well underway to set up his own general store in town. That was his dream. With everything that was going on, could he manage to provide for his beautiful bride, whom he was lucky to have, and now *two* little ones? He was not sure. It would be difficult. Finally he spoke the thought that consumed him, "Well, another mouth to feed. Gotta get back to work."

He headed out the door, but stopped and turned back to her. "Everything is going to be all right. You'll see." It was the best he could offer for the moment. Then he turned again and left the house.

Sarah cried.

She started into labor on October 16th. The valley had an early snow that year, which dumped almost two feet. James and his brothers worked all day with their father rounding up the cattle. When he came home for a quick mid-day supper, Sarah quietly announced, "I think it might be time."

"Are you sure this time?" he pressed. "I need to get back out. We have a group of lost cattle up Glenn's Canyon. They won't make it unless we bring 'em back tonight."

Actually, Sarah was not sure. She never had any children before and just the week before her discomfort led her to make the same announcement. It had been a false alarm. "Well, maybe not," she replied stoically. The labor pains were not too intense and seemed to come pretty far apart. "You go ahead. My mother and sister are here. I'm sure it'll be fine. Do hurry back, though. I still think it might be time."

Sarah felt strangely uneasy about the far away look in her husband's eyes and his stone jaw as he considered his choices. But he said gently, "I'll be back as soon as I can. It will be all right." Then he kissed her quickly and went out into the storm.

Life always seems to have an ironically perfect sense of timing. Just as it grew dark, with James still out working into the night, Sarah's water broke. She called to her mother.

"What is it, dear?" she asked as she entered Sarah's room.

"I'm not sure mother. I think my water broke. Oh, it hurts so much!"

Sarah's mother quickly assessed the situation. There was some bleeding. "Laura, come in here," she called to her younger daughter.

Sarah's sister appeared apprehensively in the doorway. "Yes, mother?"

"Go fetch Dr. Simmons," she directed. "It's time." Laura stood wide eyed and Sarah started to cry.

"Now, Laura!" She sat on the edge of the bed and took Sarah's hand. "Now it is going to be alright, dear. I know it hurts, but you will be okay. I'm just going to telephone your husband's mother. She will want to help. I'll be right here, dear."

The pain grew in intensity. James' mother and some aunts hurried over and comforted the young mother as best they could before Dr. Simmons arrived.

Sarah finally passed out, either from the pain or loss of blood, or maybe both.

They coaxed the twins into the world—James Junior (he was the oldest and they called him Jimmy) and Christopher. But meanwhile Sarah had lost a lot of blood. The grave expression on the doctor's face told the women in the room that it was serious.

"It's in God's hands now," he said in a low voice. "We need a miracle."

James came back the next afternoon. He was frightened at the sight of his wife as she lay pale and motionless, her shallow breaths barely noticeable.

Sarah finally awoke later that evening. The first thing she saw was James at her side, head buried in his hands. He looked haggard and worn-out. She could tell he'd been crying. He had come back. The thought warmed her.

"Hey, little mama," he whispered, forcing a thin smile. "You okay?"

Sarah nodded weakly. She wanted to ask him about the babies, but couldn't speak. He knew, though.

"You did a wonderful job, darling. Two big, healthy boys. All the women are taking care of them now—the babies are doing great. They'll want their mama soon. You get some sleep. Dr. Simmons says you had a close call. He'll be looking in on you soon."

It took about six weeks before Sarah could get back on her feet and took several more before she could slowly work into any sort of routine to take care of two hungry boys. She learned from Dr. Simmons just how close she came to dying. "I never saw anyone lose so much blood and come back," he said, shaking his head. "You are young and strong, so you had that going for you, but you must have had a guardian angel watching over you, pulling you through."

Sarah couldn't remember.

That Christmas, with Sarah out of commission, James took care of all the candy deliveries to the children in Marshville. But it wasn't the same.

Over time, Sarah saw James change. He took every chance he got to be apart from his growing family. He started selling goods up in the valley, which required him to be away, sometimes for weeks at a time. When he was home, he seemed grumpy, impatient and short-tempered. He loved the boys, but he acted at times like they were a big nuisance. Jimmy and Chris were too young to notice, but it about broke Sarah's heart. She couldn't talk to him about it. He'd get agitated and storm out, to go to his thinking place, she supposed. He was less affectionate with her. She didn't understand it and she couldn't get through to him.

When the twins were eighteen months old, Sarah became pregnant again. Sadly, they lost this child when she miscarried. A little girl. It was a sorrowful time. It seemed to drive James even farther away. Sarah grew even closer to the twins.

But with responsibilities to get on with, Sarah couldn't dwell on James' problems, or her own for that matter. She hired some help at the candy shop, which, by now, was riding high on its good reputation and becoming a solid business in its own right. When they were old enough, she took the boys with her and they played at her feet as she made candy or worked the sales counter. It was a wonderful, bonding time.

The Christmas right after the boys turned three was the first Christmas they were old enough to have an idea about presents and things. They were terribly excited and so was Sarah. It was fun to try to make the season special for them. James stayed sullen and silent.

They were busy, as usual, at the candy shop. More families were established in Marshville, and a little more prosperous. They could afford more sweets for the kids that year. James and Sarah felt greatly blessed and very fortunate. As usual, James did double duty taking care of his new general store and helping out with deliveries from the shop. He had the strength of an ox. He could go all day and all night, get a few hours sleep and do it all over again. This went on for the entire week before Christmas. It was a happy time, almost like it was before.

James came home early on Christmas Eve after making the final delivery. The family had a special little dinner and then their traditional program. They read and then told the Christmas story, simplifying it so the three-year olds could understand it. It was a magical evening.

They were so excited when they tacked up stockings by the fireplace. She knew they would be even more excited when they rose early in the morning. Under the tree they would find Santa brought them child-size musical instruments. James had this idea of creating a family band and he was starting them early. Sarah knew the boys would have fun with them and a few little other toys they were able to afford that year. She even found some oranges shipped up from California to put into the toes of their stockings. The smell of green pine boughs from the tree was calming and pleasant. Everyone had smiles when they put the boys to bed that night.

Sarah and James came back to the old worn sofa and sat down close to each other. James tenderly put his strong arm over her shoulder and gently drew her near to him. She laid her head on his shoulder and they both gazed upon the sprites of flame dancing in the fireplace. All the pain and heartache of the past few years were but distant memories in that sweet moment.

"Sarah, you know that I love you, don't you?"

She was pleasantly surprised. "Yes, I do know that. I love you, too."

"Do you know that you are the best thing that ever happened to me?"

Sarah didn't quite know what to say, so she tried to be light hearted. "And don't you ever forget it."

"Can I tell you something?"

"Of course you can. I'm your wife. You can tell me anything."

"Well, you might change your mind when you hear what I have to say. I wouldn't blame you. You probably won't want to live with me after I tell you, but I can't live with myself until I do."

This was all so serious. And sudden. Sarah started to get nervous. "What is it?"

"That night the twins were born. Do you remember?"

"Yes. I remember."

"It was snowing real hard. I came home for supper and you told me you were going into labor. Nothing happened and I told you I had to go back out to round up some strays. You said you would be all right, that it wouldn't happen until I got back." James dropped his eyes in shame.

"I didn't know, either, honey. They came so fast. Luckily my mother and sister were there to get help. It was just one of those things. You came to me as soon as you could." She clutched tightly to his arm. "Don't worry about it. Everything turned out just fine."

James swallowed hard. "I'm... well, I'm afraid that's not entirely true."

"What? What's not true?" She leaned away to give him a puzzled look.

"Oh, Sarah, I'm so sorry."

"James, what is it? What's wrong?"

He took a deep breath and let it out slowly. "There's no easy way to do this except come right out and say it. That night I went back out like I told you. I caught up with my brothers about an hour later. Turns out they'd already found the strays and brought them in. I could have come home then, but I didn't."

Sarah couldn't believe what she was hearing. "What do you mean, James? What did you do?" she asked numbly.

"Well, I was scared, Sarah. Scared of becoming a new father. Scared of losing you. Scared they would be twins. Scared of birth. Scared. I was scared." James speech became clipped and high-pitched as he relived his feelings. Then, more quietly he continued, "And so, instead of turning back and coming home, I headed into town."

"To town?" she blankly asked.

"I lied to my brothers and told them I had a delivery up White Lake way, and then was going to get the doctor. I met up with the Hatch boys and we went to the tavern. I went drinking, Sarah. While you were giving birth to our sons, I was getting drunk."

"What do you mean? James, you don't drink." Sarah was totally confused.

"I never did before and haven't since, but that night I passed out, Sarah. I didn't even wake up until the next afternoon. When I came home and found out you might die, I cried. I couldn't stand myself, what I had done to you, to our boys, to myself. No one knew, of course. And for three years, I let you think I was out all night working hard."

"You abandoned me?"

James bowed his headed shamefully and nodded. "I'm sorry. I know you must hate me. I'm prepared to accept that. I'm not much of a man. You deserve so much better."

"I ... I don't know what to say."

"I have to be honest with you, Sarah. You're too good a woman to lie to. I know this hurts. I won't blame you if you kick me out and get a divorce. But you have to know." Tears trickled down his cheeks.

In that moment, she did hate him. A man's job, if it was anything, was to protect his wife and family and he simply left her because he was afraid! What a coward! She despised him for his weakness. She despised him for lying to her and his brothers and sons. She despised his allowing himself to be thought of as something of a hero these past three years when he was really just the opposite. She despised him for his cold detachment from his sons and her since that day. She despised him that he betrayed her trust in him. Yes, Sarah intensely hated James. She'd almost died! If not for their mothers and aunts and sisters, along with Dr. Simmons, she would have.

"Why did you have to tell me this on Christmas Eve, of all times?" Sarah's wounded heart cried. A rushing river of viciousness raged through her. She wanted to hurt him like he had hurt her. She wanted him to suffer. She wished she *had* died that day. She wished now that he would die. How could she live with a man who had done such a thing to her? How could she ever trust him again? "We can't go on," she thought. "I am betrayed. He has to pay. For the twins' sake, he can stay through the morning, but then he will have to go. Where to, I do not care."

Just as Sarah was ready to give in to the urge to make that biting, spiteful ultimatum, the flickering firelight illuminated the little nativity scene set up on the lamp table. She paused. Her eye was drawn to the tiny bed of the child whose birth they celebrated.

Something happened next that Sarah could not explain, something glorious and transcendent. In her mind's eye, she saw the child who as a man would also be abandoned and betrayed. He, too, was wounded. He, too, hurt and suffered, and finally he died. In her mind she vividly pictured him kneeling before God, crying out, sweating in great agony for the burden of all mankind.

Only, now came the understanding it wasn't just for all mankind. It was for her—Sarah Daly Williams. The paradox that his gift was universal and, at once, so personal, overwhelmed her with amazement. She realized that even if she were the only soul who ever needed it, he would have still gone through it all.

Just for her.

Suddenly, with awful horror, Sarah woke up to the fact that it was her pain, her hurt, her anger and sense of betrayal that an innocent child who grew up to be the Innocent Man had already long ago absorbed. He had already felt all that she now felt, and many times more. He had already paid for it with his own life. There was no need for Sarah Williams to carry the burden and feel the suffering all over again.

"Joy to the world, the Lord is come." The words of the song rang in her head. "Let earth receive her King." Could she do it? Could she receive her King?

He was the Forgiver. She now realized that since He had forgiven James, it was not her prerogative not to do so.

The scene in Sarah's mind changed. She was the petitioner now. Now it was her head bowed in shameful contrition. Instead of her miserable husband begging for forgiveness from her, she was earnestly pleading for mercy from One to whom she owed the greatest of all debts.

"Forgive us our debts as we forgive our debtors ..." She was face to face with the lesson she rotely recited so often in her youth. She knew then what she must do.

Ready to respond, Sarah calmly looked upon the pitiful figure of her sobbing husband.

"You are right, James. You did a weak, cowardly thing. You don't deserve me." She reached over and took his hand. This would be the hardest thing she had yet to do, even when compared to that night and the following days in October three years ago. "Look at me, James."

James raised his wet, red eyes, expecting the worst.

"I love you. I don't know how right now, but we'll get through this thing. The only thing I do know is that I have to somehow forgive this thing you have done. I will forget it. As far as I'm concerned, you need never mention it again. I do forgive you. I will not bring it up and I hope you do not bring it up again. I want our marriage to be bigger than this thing. Our family is more important than this thing. We'll get through it."

He wept. She wept. They hugged each other tightly. They prayed. If the Lord himself were sitting there in front of that flickering fire, they could not have felt any closer to Him. It was a turning point, a purifying moment when all in their universe seemed connected and right. That Christmas Eve the Christ was born anew, this time in the hearts of a struggling young couple, James and Sarah Williams.

They vowed that night that nothing would be so big that they would not forgive each other, nor anything so small that they would not beg forgiveness of each other.

And that's a promise they kept.

കൃ

Tuesday, March 12.

I visited Sarah Williams again today. Every time I visit I feel like I enter as a dry sponge and come out dripping wet, full of her wisdom and life. I just love her!

Anyway, I always learn so much in visiting her. On the other hand, I have so much to learn, like that my small and petty problems are hardly worth bringing up. It puts things in perspective for me.

I'm beginning to understand how she and James were so close. Anytime their relationship was knicked or wounded by anything big or small, they applied a liberal dose of a special healing balm. It let them unburden their souls.

Healthy souls make for healthy relationships.

I think that some pretend they have no wounds and cover up their guilt with anger or depression or a disconnected marriage. James and Sarah had a medicine that healed and changed things for the better.

She said what they did was to spread it on every time anything came up, any misunderstanding, unintended offense, any insensitive act by either of them. They added another big dose on Christmas Eve, whether they needed it or not. Part of their tradition of love. It helped them remember.

She said the ingredients of the healing balm recipe are simple: a tablespoon of forgiveness, a double tablespoon of letting go, and a generous pinch of forgetting...

That is the Second Secret: Forgive. Let go. Leave it alone.

Chapter Four

Remember who you are, and miracles will happen.

The remaining days of March dragged by slowly that year for Corinne. The gray, overcast daytime skies matched the mood brooding in her soul. It seemed rain or snow fell nearly every day. She didn't know why, but heaviness clouded her heart, a drooping sadness that often left her lethargic. She had to figure out some way to shake this thing, to support Ed through his struggles to provide for them while finding meaning and happiness in her own daily activity.

Some days were better than others, of course, but overall she just couldn't get rid of her dark feelings. They weren't the black sort of dark, just a gray uneasiness about something hanging invisibly around her. To make things worse, she caught some sort of bug the last week of the month and spent a good deal of time getting acquainted with the annoying interruptions of nausea. She hated being sick.

Or miserable.

Or alone.

The brighter days of April could not come too soon for Corrine Whitmore.

Edward's work was very demanding. But he did make an honest attempt to cut down the long hours and to pay more attention to his wife. He figured it was like keeping his Chevrolet in top condition. You had to perform certain maintenance chores in a marriage if you wanted it to keep running smoothly. He realized he wasn't spending enough time with Corinne, and so he tried to make a point of getting home earlier from his office.

The problem was that even when he was home, he still thought about work. There had been a few snags along the way. Ed's company needed more money to fully advance the motor inn cabins concept. If it was to be the tourism draw they envisioned it would be, the development had to be done right. It had to be big and daring, something that would pull people in and cause them to stay for a night.

The expenses, however, were piling up and delays were costly. They had planned well, but they were running out of money. The lenders were not convinced pouring more money into the enterprise would help. Without some assurances, they would not sign on to the idea. Until more of them did, his group could not pry free the sufficient funds to move things forward.

Tom Perkins, Ed's boss, realized they had a sales job to do in the community. They needed other local merchants to support them. After all, more tourists meant more business for them all. Most owners were behind the idea, but there were still some skeptics. And so their timetable was pushed back at least two, maybe three months. Ed was optimistic the doubters would eventually be persuaded. It would just take a little longer, that's all.

Meanwhile, his insurance sales were suffering. His commissions had dropped off and for the first time in their marriage the money was just barely covering their bills. Ed's instinct was to work even harder, to spend even more time hunting for sales. And that meant more time away from his wife. He had to figure out some way to see more people, make more sales and now, in addition, beat the bushes for critical support for the project. Oh, yes, and find time for Corinne. The pressure was on.

So it became a tricky balancing act for both of them.

One evening in mid April, Ed came home on time, which was a good start. Corinne greeted him in her usual fashion with a

"Hello, dear," followed by a kiss, which in turn was followed by a "How was your day?"

"It was fine. How was yours?" came the routine reply.

"It was good. Supper will be ready in a few minutes."

Ed hung up his hat and coat in the small entry closet, and then went to wash his hands. Corinne moved back into the kitchen to finish fixing the food.

This was their ritual every night that Ed didn't have to stay late to work.

They came to the table when the food was ready and had a blessing. "I'm starving tonight," Ed said as he placed a napkin in his lap. "We had meetings right through lunch today, so I haven't had anything since breakfast."

He reached eagerly for a covered dish and removed the lid. Steam escaped in happy circles above their heads. Corinne had prepared a nice supper consisting of new potatoes and green peas in smooth white gravy, roast beef left over from Sunday's dinner, hot rolls, and peach jam she and her mother put up last fall. Ed spooned a big helping of the potato-peas dish onto his plate.

"Nothing since breakfast! You poor dear," Corinne sympathized.

Ed enjoyed the pity and attention. "Well, this looks wonderful and will more than make up for it, I'm sure."

Corinne felt warm satisfaction. "Did the meeting go well?"

"Pretty well," Ed replied. He was eating quickly, but put down his fork so that he could use his hands to make his next points. "We made great progress with most of the merchants we need on our side to get things moving again with our investors. All but two are either in support or at least won't fight it now."

"That's good, isn't it?"

"I suppose." He picked up his fork and stabbed into a large morsel of roast beef.

"Who are the last two?" Corinne asked as she daintily picked at her food.

Ed waited until he finished chewing. "Well, one of them is Willie Martin at Martin's Garage and Gasoline. You know the place, just over there on 3rd Avenue where it intersects with Highway 30?"

"Yes. Kind of a stubborn, stern old fellow, isn't he?"

"Stubborn? Stern? That's like calling the Rocky Mountains a bump in the road. He's absolutely obstinate."

"Yes, I met him once. His daughter Geraldine—you remember Geraldine, from my high school class?"

"Yeah, barely. When you were sophomores and I was a senior. But you were the only one who really caught my eye," Ed replied. Corinne smiled. "Let's see. Dark hair. A little on the short side?"

"Yes, and extremely smart, too. Went with Tim Burroughs. Anyway, she took me over to her daddy's garage one day after school. He hollered and cursed at her about something. She had to get down under a dirty old car and do something he was upset about. He scared me something awful."

"Sounds like the man. Can't reason with the fellow. He's too narrow-minded. Not narrow. Closed-minded."

"I felt sorry for Geraldine, with her mother dying when she was just nine and having to live with that mean old man."

"You mean her father."

"He was still a mean, old man."

"Didn't she run off with that drifter her father hired as a mechanic a few years back?"

"No, that's just hurtful gossip and you shouldn't repeat it." Corinne scolded. "Her daddy made sure nothing like that happened. He chased that rascal out of town. Geraldine ended up going to college down south somewhere. Did real well, too. Studying law, or so I heard."

Ed raised his eyebrows in surprise. "No kidding?" Most young people could only dream of making it outside of the valley. Few ever did. For a girl to try was unheard of in these parts. "Well, anyway, old Willie Martin is against the project because he thinks it will raise taxes and he's dead set against the government taking one nickel more out of his pocket."

"Will they?"

"Will they what?"

"Raise taxes?"

"Of course not," Ed said forcefully. "At least not under our proposal. Now there's some legislator from a county on the western side of the state who's talking about a tax increase on commercial developments of this type." Ed sounded more like he was in front of the mayor and city council than with his wife at the supper table. "He wants to pay for paving and upkeep of roads with the extra money. That's too anti-business to make it very far, though. It'll never fly."

"But if it does, his taxes might go up?" Corinne persisted.

"Willie Martin could fly to the moon sooner than he'd pay more taxes just because of new business development," Ed puffed. "Anyway, he benefits directly from all the improvements. He just hasn't made the connection that the improvements will help us attract a lot more tourists to the valley. More tourists mean more traffic, more traffic means more cars that will need gasoline and service. And most of those cars will be moving down Highway 30, right past Martin's Garage and Gasoline. He could make a killing."

"So why won't he support it?"

"He will eventually. He may be a crank, but he's no fool," Ed said confidently. "He likes to make a buck too much to let this chance pass by. It's the other one we're a little more worried about, though."

"Who's that?"

"Williams' General."

"The mercantile set up by James and Sarah Williams?"

"That's the one."

"But they're not even close to the highway. Why on earth would they object?"

"That's what we can't quite figure out. All we get from current management is something about a commitment."

"A commitment?"

"Yeah." Ed furrowed his brow and rubbed his right temple. The strain was obvious. "A few years before James Williams passed away, with their children gone and everything, they asked the Thompson family to manage the enterprise. They've been helping the Williams almost from the start. Ben Thompson runs the place now. He's a progressive kind of guy—has modernized and patterned his place after some of the big department stores back East. That's why I can't figure him. All he'll tell us is he can't go along with us because of a commitment."

"What kind of commitment?"

"He didn't exactly say."

"Why doesn't your group just go ahead without his endorsement?"

Ed was irritated by the question. Irritated because it scratched too close to the surface of failure. What did his wife know about business deals? Who did she think she was? He masked his own doubts with a condescending, patronizing reply.

"It's not that simple. My boss, Mr. Perkins, goes way back with the Williams and Thompsons. Those are influential names around here, you know. And if we push ahead, they'll fight us on it. We'd rather not have to face that."

They had finished eating and Ed pushed his chair away from the supper table.

"A fight like that would split this town. It would bring the project down. If only Ben would talk to us, I'm sure …"

Corinne saw Ed's irritation and how he was getting all worked up in his frustration about the deal. Time to change the subject. "Let's do these dishes." It was more a plea for help than a demand. She wouldn't complain to Ed, but she was tired, not feeling all that well again today.

Ed paused and looked at his wife. "Sure," he said and piled the silverware on his plate.

CЗ

A week and a half later, Corinne visited Sarah Williams.

"Your feet are like icicles today," Corinne noted after she had proficiently completed her trimming and filing. She gently took the left one and gently began massaging it between her palms.

"Oh my, that's simply heavenly, my dear," the old woman sighed.

Corinne smiled as she continued rubbing. She looked up into Sarah's face. There was beauty and a glow radiating a youthfulness that belied her many years. She wondered about the secret of Sarah's perpetual beauty. Probably genetic, she thought.

Corinne also saw tears trickling from the old woman's eyes. "Mrs. Williams, is something the matter? Am I rubbing too hard? Am I hurting you?"

"No. No. Please, you are doing a masterful job. Everything is splendid. I'm touched by your extremely kind service, that's all. Do you understand?"

Corinne hadn't thought about it before because of the need in her that fulfilled each time she was with Sarah Williams. "I think I do," she replied.

"It's just that I am so happy you've come again to visit. I can always count on you, can't I?"

Corinne nodded. "Of course you can!" She rubbed and rubbed, moving from the instep and top to the ankle and down to the heel, then along the bottom arch to the toes. Gradually, with the circulation stimulated, she could feel the warmth return to Mrs. Williams' left foot. So she began tenderly working the right one.

"You're the only visitor who ever comes over anymore," Sarah lamented. "Unless you count Ben Thompson who runs the store and comes over to give me business reports. And Doc Crandall. But he just comes around to fuss at me about my medicine, the old quack."

"I'm sure he's just trying to look after you," Corinne suggested.

"He's trying to push me into my grave, is what he's trying to do, with all his pills and potions," Sarah retorted. "Anyway, I'm old enough by now to have figured out how to take care of myself without some grouchy old country doctor trying to change me. He comes to bother, not to visit."

Corinne chuckled. "Well, at least he's kept you feisty enough to fuss back at him."

Sarah laughed. The foot massage seemed to relax her entire body. She leaned back in her overstuffed chair and blissfully closed her eyes. After a moment she opened them again and earnestly leaned forward. "My Maggie is out in California with her husband Paul and the kids. Grandkids now, too! Peter's in California, but down in the southern part. A long ways from Maggie. And Merlin and Sheryl are out in Boston." Sarah looked earnestly at Corinne. "You know, dear, without you, I don't know what I would do."

Corinne knew she didn't really do very much. "Well, I enjoy our visits, Mrs. Williams. I really do. I learn a lot from you when I come." It dawned on Corinne that maybe she should come by more than once a month.

"You won't stop will you? Coming to visit me, I mean?"

"Not until you want me to," Corinne answered.

"Will you promise me?"

Corinne felt uncomfortable with the old woman's intensity. Would she promise? She contemplated the commitment being asked. It seemed large at the moment. Could she really continue to stop by faithfully every month? What if she got busy or sick or something? Wasn't there at least a distant family member of some sort who should be looking in on her, taking care of her, meeting her needs? Wasn't there someone down at the church who was more experienced, who should help out and keep Sarah from becoming so lonely? She liked the old woman and wanted to visit her. But a promise?

"Yes, I promise," Corinne finally said.

Sarah leaned back and closed her eyes once more. "I knew I could count on you. I knew it." Then, after a short pause, she added, "You know, Corinne Whitmore, you are an extraordinarily marvelous person. Do you know that?"

Corinne felt embarrassed and did not know quite what to say. "Oh, Mrs. Williams, there's nothing much marvelous about me."

"Oh, but there is. There have been many girls grow up in this town, some are gone, a few still around. But you are special. You may not see it in yourself, but others do. I do. I'm sure your husband does."

"I'm not too sure about that," Corinne responded, thinking of Ed's absorption with what seemed like everything else except her.

"Now, now. Of course he does," Sarah insisted. With the quiet wisdom borne of age she added, "He may not show it yet in the just the way you want and you may not understand what he really, deep down sees in you. Be patient, dear. In time, you'll both catch on. Meanwhile, remember who you are."

"Remember who I am?"

"Yes, child."

"What do you mean?"

Sarah searched for a way to help her young visitor understand. "Years ago, when he was about seven or eight years old I guess, our fourth son Peter brought a quart-size tin cooking pot filled with dirt into the house. He proudly presented it to me and announced it was his special gift to me. 'It's a flower,' he confidently told me. 'You have to water it and put it in the sun. Then it will grow!' This was after we moved up from Marshville. James was still adding on to some parts of the house then, but the kitchen was all done. So, to humor Peter, I put that pot of dirt on the window sill, just back in that room behind us here." Sarah waved her arm in the direction of the kitchen.

Corinne imagined the sweet picture and smiled.

"To me it was just a pot of dirt. I didn't really know if anything would grow in it or not. Even if something did grow I figured it would be some weed Peter dug up from the fields nearby. But he was so excited and so sincere ... So, I put it there at the window and waited for him to forget all about it. Then I'd just dump the dirt out, you see, and get my pot back."

"Did anything ever grow?" Corinne asked curiously.

"Well, you know, that little boy of mine checked every single day for weeks. Nothing happened. Until one day he came running, all excited. 'It's happening! It's happening!' Sure enough, when he took me to look at that little pot in the windowsill, a little green shoot had popped up through the dirt. Something was growing, but what it was we couldn't tell. Peter insisted it was going to be a beautiful flower. I couldn't see it, though. I still thought it was probably some milkweed or a dandelion or something."

"And was it?" Corinne wanted to know.

"It was a little miracle, is what it was. That tiny plant turned out to be a tulip of all things! With beautiful, velvety red petals. Don't ask me where a young boy came up with a tulip bulb. We never found out for certain. He was always going over to the Poulsen's who had a dairy just north of town. They had all kinds of flowers growing up there. We figured maybe that's where he got it."

Corinne loved flowers. She remembered planting some bulbs just last fall at her mother's place. Daffodils mostly, but a few tulips, too. They were just now coming into bloom. Many homes in the valley had them. Her plan for the coming fall was to separate and transplant some at her own home, now that she and Ed were married.

"We replanted that bulb outside the house. Semi-shade, of course, where it would bloom later and last longer. You need soil with good drainage, too, or your bulbs will get too wet."

"I didn't know that," Corinne said.

"Yes, you need to be careful of that," Sarah affirmed. "We planted a lot more over the years. Added some irises and begonias and daisies. Petunias. Tried roses, too. But the tulips from Peter's start were the best if you ask me."

The old woman sat up in her chair struggling slowly to rise. "Excuse me for a moment. Time to take my medicine. Don't want that old sourpuss Doc Crandall fussing at me."

"I'll get it for you," Corinne offered. "You just stay put. Where do you keep it?"

"The pills in the bottle by the kitchen sink. I take two of them three times a day. They're probably killing me, but it's too late to worry about that now, don't you agree?"

Corinne smiled and hurried to the kitchen. It was a homey place. Neat and tidy with lots of old-fashioned implements in their places. A needlepoint hung on the wall. It looked to Corinne like a family tree with generations of names appearing on green-leafed branches. Another was framed and hung right beside it. It had musical instruments embroidered around the edges with a saying in the middle. It read, "Music is the poetry of the soul." She readily found the bottle, removed two pills and returned with a glass of water. Sarah Williams swallowed each with a quick sip from the glass. She set it down on the small table beside her and motioned for Corinne to sit down again.

"Anyway, as I was saying, dear, I think you're a pot of dirt."

"I beg your pardon?"

"… with a beautiful flower planted inside," Sarah continued. "Just be patient. One day you'll bloom in breathtaking splendor and everyone will recognize you for the remarkable soul that you are."

"Well, I'm pretty average. If it ever actually happens, it will certainly take a long time," Corinne noted doubtfully.

"Time means nothing when dealing with eternity," Sarah responded. "Peter's gift was a simple, childish offering. But he could see something I couldn't. He saw a gorgeous flower when all the rest of us could see only a pot of dirt. The interesting thing is, the tulip was a tulip all along. It was what it was while yet a bulb sleeping with potential in that dented old pot. It was a tulip when sending forth its little green shoot on the windowsill. It was a tulip when finally in full bloom, obvious then to all of us. And it was a tulip when its petals dropped from its drooping stalk and the tips of its leaves turned brown and withered. Peter was right. It was what it was. It was always a beautiful tulip."

Corinne pondered Sarah's words. They rested true and easy on her soul, like the gentle spring sun kindly thawing the cold grasp of winter's tyranny. She straightened her posture, quivering with excitement at the awakening now dawning upon her. Remember who you are. Oh, if only she could remember. She felt something—a vague recollection... But remember what? From when? From where?

"Mrs. Williams?" she ventured tentatively.

"Please. Would you call me Sarah, dear. I would like that."

"Okay. Sarah, is there really ... I mean ..." Corinne stopped, suddenly too embarrassed to go on.

She didn't need to. The old woman stretched out her hand to Corinne in an inviting gesture, motioning for her to move to her side. "Come here, dear."

Corinne got up off the sofa and kneeled next to Sarah Williams' chair. The old woman clasped the younger girl's hand and firmly cupped it in both of hers. She looked resolutely into Corinne's eyes.

"Let me tell you something. This memory about yourself is not up here," Sarah said pointing to her head. "It's in here." She placed a hand on her heart. "I want you to listen to what I have to say. The sooner you figure these things out, the better. It took me quite a few years to learn what I'm going to tell you. I wish I'd known them when I was your age."

Corinne was eager to hear whatever wisdom the most beloved and highly respected woman of the valley might impart to her today.

It amazed her when she thought of it, to grasp that someone as young and inexperienced as she was could actually be spending time in the company of someone like Mrs. Williams. To be invited to learn from her in such an intimate way was a great honor. It was more than an honor. It became an obligation, a commitment to drink as deeply as possible from the reservoir of sagacity now opened to her. Corinne might have been intimidated, but the old woman's kindly demeanor and warm spirit helped Corinne feel comfortable and relaxed. She shifted her weight into a sitting position on the floor, curling her legs under her and wrapping her skirt over her knees. Still holding Sarah's hand, Corinne was ready to listen.

"The first thing to remember is that you and I and James and Edward and everyone ever born of women into this big world are each a child of God."

This was not what Corinne expected. She had heard that before. She was taught it at the white church building over on Fourth Street all her life, for as long as she could remember. It was almost a trite saying to her. A child of God? So what? Where did that get her? Nevertheless, she nodded and said, "Yes. I believe that."

"Do you?" Sarah gently challenged. She reached for her glass and took another sip of water. "You know, not everyone believes that anymore. There is this idea gaining in popularity that mankind evolved over many years from lower animal life."

"We're not animals!" The passion with which Corinne said it burst forth like waters from a broken dam. From her sitting position on the floor, her back became indignantly erect.

Sarah smiled gently. "Well, dear, I agree. Some of the ideas get a bit puzzling."

"Yes, I know. I am not sure about the science behind evolution," Corinne said, relaxing a little. "I've read about it. And I read about that trial in Dayton, Tennessee that happened a few years back—the John Scopes trial? But I am confused by it, to tell the truth."

Sarah paused a moment. "When I don't understand how a theory or idea or thought matches what I know to be true, do you know what I've learned to do?"

"What?"

"I just put it on a shelf in my mind, like a jar of bottled fruit in the pantry. Every now and again, I take it down off the shelf, dust it off, and examine it to see if it has changed any or contributes in any way to making me a better person. If it has, I open it up and use it. If not, I just put it back up on the shelf and don't worry about it. Sometimes I realize there are some ideas that are just worthless clutter and should be thrown away. So I do."

"And is the theory of evolution one those?"

"You'll have to come to your own conclusions," Sarah smiled.

"That makes sense to me," Corinne nodded. "But how could anyone think we are just animals?"

"Well, all I can say is I happen to believe that the most damaging and darkest idea that we have in the world is that we are not children of a loving Heavenly Father."

Sarah's words were reassuring to Corinne.

"You know, James and I had five boys. Peter and Merlin are the only ones left now. They live far away. One on the west coast—that's Peter—and Merlin's out on the east coast. They're old men with grandchildren of their own." Sarah shook her head in disbelief. The generations were passing her too rapidly these days. "Anyway, every one of our five boys had a beautiful thick head of shiny black hair just like their father. They had his eyes and smile, too. Handsome just like their father, every one of them."

"Didn't you have a girl, too?"

"Maggie, our baby. She took after me, her mother—you know, very pretty and talented."

Corrine glanced at the old woman. Sarah grinned as if she had made a good joke. "In fact, they were all musically gifted. We had this family band from the time the children were old enough to pick up instruments."

Sarah stopped speaking, something caught in her throat. She took another sip of water. "We were good. It was a wonderful experience. Great memories of that family band. It was one of the best things to happen to us."

"I wish I had been around to hear you," Corinne said.

"Yes. Well, the point is, those children inherited something from their father and me. It's genetics."

"I understand," Corinne replied.

"I have this notion that each one of God's children inherits just a little bit of his divine nature. Some get the gift of love like you. Others get a gift of faith or of wisdom or any number of other gifts. It's genetics. But instead of physical, these are spiritual genes. Children grow up to be like their parents. Do you see what we are meant to be? Can you think of that now and again when you remember who you are?"

"Is that really true? That I … I mean we, are daughters of God who loves us and cares about us?"

"I've lived long enough and experienced enough to know that it is true. I know that in spiritual ways He will reveal Himself to you, if you seek Him. What's more interesting is that, over time, he will reveal *yourself* to you."

Corinne's mind raced with new insight, scarcely able to keep up with the old woman.

"James was a wonderful father to all the children," Sarah continued. She grew wistful, gazed off into space and grew momentarily silent.

"Fact is, the family band was his idea, and they responded wonderfully well to him. Now of course, when they had small questions or problems like where to find a pair of socks or something, they'd always run to me with it. I'd give them directions or bandage a hurt and kiss it and make it better. But when they had real questions, James was the one they'd go to. He was approachable for them that way, even if he was busy. So, you see, when you understand that you actually are a daughter of a loving Heavenly Father, you will not find it difficult to go to Him for answers."

It was a large idea of colossal importance. She, Corinne Johnson Whitmore, a daughter of God destined to be like her divine parent, endowed with divine gifts, able to rise above the petty and small and mean. Was that who she really was? It would take some time to sink in. If true, she knew it would take a lifetime and longer to fulfill the potential it suggested.

Sarah pointed to some books on a shelf near the entry to the sitting room. "There's a volume over there I'd like you to get. Would you be so kind as to bring it to me? It's titled *History of White Lake Valley Pioneers*. Do you see it there?"

Corinne looked quickly up and down the massive bookcase. Finally she spotted the book, leather-bound, gold-colored lettering. "Yes, here it is." She carried it back to Sarah's side.

"Now where are my reading glasses?" Sarah wondered aloud, searching her memory for a connection that would not come.

"Are these the ones?" Corinne asked. They had been on the lamp table next to Sarah, behind the glass of water.

"Oh, yes, thank you, dear." Sarah took off her seeing glasses, as she called them, and put the reading glasses on her nose. Then she reached for the book and with frail fingers turned pages until she was about a third of the way into the thick volume. "Yes. Here we are. The Frank Daly Family. That was my father. His wife Mary Ellen MacGregor was my mother. They were one of the first settlers in the valley near the town of Marshville where I was born."

Corinne was fascinated. "This is wonderful! Where did you get a book like this?"

"The Daughters of the Western Pioneers published it a few years ago. Just after the turn of the century. My goodness, that was twenty-five or thirty years ago now. I lose track of time these days. I am a member of the DWP society, you know, and happened to be president when we got this thing put together. They thought they had to give me a fancy edition, but I would have been happy enough with a regular cloth-bound book."

"Where can I get one of these?" Corinne asked enthusiastically.

"I'll see what I can do," Sarah promised. "Now I would like you to read this to me, would you please?"

Corinne took the book and began at the spot pointed out by Sarah. Her father wrote it.

> *My fishing and hunting experiences commenced in 1857, by taking a 13-pound trout from Mars Creek. When fishing on the lake I used 140 seine and a boat. In May, 80 large trout and a few other fish were removed from the seine at a landing near the mouth of Eagle Creek. During this time I was sending fish to Green Valley, St. Charles, Mountain View and New Leicester City.*
>
> *Beaver were so numerous that a trapper could average four every day, but four head of elk was the most I ever killed in one day and I remember killing nine deer in one day. In the forepart of winter of 1875, I bagged 56 deer. I have captured and killed 109 bear in my time. It has been five years since I trapped a Silver Tip in Jamestown Canyon. The hide measured ten feet in length and we took 23 gallons of oil from this animal.*
>
> *I am now past 80 years and Mrs. Daly says the reason I am not bald is because I have used so much bear oil in my hair. We often have doughnuts fried in bear oil and find it useful in many other ways. I never happened to get mixed up in a bear fight, being too cowardly. Before removing the hide, I always tried to be quite sure the bear was dead.*

"This is marvelous!" Corinne exclaimed when she finished the passage. "Look. It says here "the people of Marshville owe a great deal to Mr. and Mrs. Frank Daly and their family. Mr. Daly played the violin and Mrs. Daly taught dancing to all the young people." And it says here that he "taught all his sons and daughters to play musical instruments and his daughters to dance and sing.""

"So now you know who I am a little bit more by knowing something of where I came from," Sarah said reflectively. "Dad died just after the turn of the century. June of 1901. He lived to be a very old man. Mother died thirteen years before him. He was very strict. But Mother could always bring out the softer side in him. He was always a perfect gentleman and she was an elegant lady when out in society."

"What was your mother like?" Corinne wanted to know.

"An amazing woman. Simply amazing. She had eleven children, four boys and seven of us girls. Three of my siblings passed away before childhood. Two of them before I was born. I was number seven, you know. But I do remember my baby sister, who lived just a few weeks before passing on from chills and fever. Tore my mother up. I remember her tears rolling down the cheeks of that baby as she hugged her child one last time before giving her up to be buried. I was six years old at the time, but I remember her tears like it happened yesterday. She raised us to work hard and be respectful of others and to treat others less fortunate with compassion and kindness. She was amazing."

Sarah became thoroughly engrossed in reminiscing about her family. She spoke of her mother teaching children and adults to read. She spoke of grandfathers and grandmothers, aunts and uncles and cousins. She spoke of ancestors whose lives were spent in times and places far removed from Sarah and Corinne that April afternoon. She gained strength and vigor and light as she spoke. A glow came into her countenance that the pores of her skin could not hold back, and Sarah radiated her happiness in remembering.

Corinne, for her part, was enchanted by Sarah's tales about her family. It seemed she was the audience in a theatrical production with a colorful cast of characters, each with a thrilling tale to tell. Each would take a bow and then turn life's stage over to another member of the family. The climax of the production, in Corinne's mind, came in the person of Sarah Daly Williams, the recipient of a rich heritage of hope and legacy of love, a treasure chest of gifts accumulated over centuries of living and giving.

"Never neglect your roots," Sarah concluded. "Your roots will determine your fruits. Honor your family name. Remember who you are and miracles will happen."

"I see what you mean," Corinne nodded. There was much to consider: a spiritual heritage from a loving Heavenly Father coupled with a family heritage from generations on whose shoulders she now stood indeed defined her foundations.

"Of course, who you really are shows up in what you do with all the gifts you've been given," Sarah added. She launched into what was her last story of an afternoon that, for Corinne, flew by all too quickly.

ॐ

James stomped into the house fuming. The hairs of his thick mustache trapped a layer of fresh snow, but the heat of his temper quickly melted it. His face was red. He didn't swear, but he sure felt like doing it. "I can't believe it! I just can't believe it!" he fairly hollered.

Sarah quickly met him in the doorway and helped remove the heavy coat from his broad, muscular shoulders. "Shhh. The children, James. Whatever it is, I'm sure it will be all right."

"That drunken, good-for-nothing, disgrace of a man has done it again!" he squawked. Then Sarah's reminder about the children being within earshot registered and James began to compose himself. "I'm sorry. It's just that somebody needs to do something."

"You mean Parker Thompson," Sarah said in a quiet voice.

James nodded and began removing the soggy, cold boots from his feet. "Yes, yes. Parker Thompson. Again. Ever since we moved up here from Marshville we've had problems with that … that … poor excuse of a man." James almost swore again. "Somebody needs to horsewhip some sense into that devil, and, by heaven, I'll be the first to volunteer."

"Lower your voice, James," Sarah cautioned, ever protective of the children's sensibilities. "Let me just finish putting Maggie to bed and I'll get your supper. Then you tell me what happened this time."

James and Sarah tucked their children in bed after prayers. The boys shared a large bedroom upstairs; Maggie had a room all to herself, she being the youngest and the only girl. The whole thing took about twenty minutes. Then they went into the kitchen where Sarah brought her husband his food as he sat down at the table.

James quickly polished off his favorite late evening meal of bread and milk while Sarah watched. "Parker took our money he collected on delivery. Forty dollars. Went over to Mountain View again," he began.

Mountain View was about twelve miles north east of White Lake, at the base of the mountains. It was a rough town, established decades before by an enterprising scoundrel known as "Peg Leg" Brown. Looking to make a fast buck, he set up a trading post/saloon with booze and cards and loose women to service the adventurous travelers passing through on their way to the West Coast. The scheme prospered, but after a few years, "Peg Leg" himself was seduced by the promise of gold and easy riches and took off for California. The local folks never heard from him again. The saloon stayed, however. Now Mountain View stood in sharp contrast to the orderly neighboring towns in the valley filled with honest, hard-working families. It was one of the few places in the entire valley where liquor by the drink was served. It was the only place where gambling occurred.

"Oh no," Sarah sympathized.

"Yep, that rascal. Two twenty dollar gold pieces, I'm sure. That's the way Patterson's always pays and that's where I sent him today with a wagonload of goods. Squandered it all on drinking and gambling, no doubt." James was once more visibly agitated. "I've got to fire him. We can't afford to keep someone like that when we're trying to get the store established in this new place."

"But James, what about his wife? And those poor little babies? And just a few days before Christmas like this. I feel so sorry for them."

"He's brought it on himself. The scoundrel is *stealing* from us, Sarah," James emphasized. "And then he just drinks it away. It's not like he's using it to put food on his table. How many times does this make now? Five? Six?"

"This is the third, Sarah corrected, "and the first in a long time. Who else would you get to make our traditional Christmas deliveries? I don't think now is the time to make a decision about letting him go."

"Are you sure it's only the third? Seems like more than that," James grumbled. "He's worthless. He's more than worthless. Someone who's worthless merely adds zero to the business. Not zero, he's subtracting. This man is costing us. He takes away, creates a negative balance. I pity his family, too. Lord knows I've been more than patient trying to help the man. But I've got to watch out for my own and he's hurting my ability to provide for you all. It isn't right. I can't afford to risk it any longer."

"He's still a good man," Sarah protested. "With the right chance, I think he'd turn himself around."

"Nah, he's too wrapped up in himself, too greedy and greed always slows down a growing enterprise." James was firm in his resolve. He was a man of action, after all, and the time had come to act. Yes, he was patient and principled. He tried as much as anyone to give a fellow a fair shake. But Parker had used up his chances as far as he was concerned.

Sarah was just as firm in her resolve. "He's still a good man," she repeated.

James continued to vent. "I was counting on him to help out with the candy deliveries this Christmas up here in White Lake. I was going to go down for a day or to Marshville, look in on our store there, and help with the traditional deliveries to some of our old friends and families back there. That's completely out of the question now. I'm going to have to stay up here and do it all myself."

"We've got Tom Wilcox running things in Marshville. Leave it to him."

"I know. I just wanted to get back. Tradition and all of that, you know. Dang that Parker's hide!"

"Let him help you out up here," Sarah insisted. "Deep down I know he wants to do right."

"He's a sot. He's chained to the bottle."

"He can change."

James let out a deep sigh of exasperation. "It's no use, Sarah. My mind's made up. He's had too many chances. He's proved he can't change."

Sarah said nothing. She was often powerful when silent.

James grew uncomfortable. "Well, what in heaven's name do you expect me to do!" he bellowed. "Look at the facts. He was drunk. He took the delivery payment and gambled it away. And it's just before Christmas! And this is the fourth time!"

"Third," Sarah corrected.

"All right, third!" James pounded a clenched fist on the table for emphasis. "What I should do...I think I'll swear out a warrant for his arrest first thing in the morning. It's the only way to get through to someone like Parker Thompson. I won't be turned on this, Sarah."

Still she said nothing.

James ran his fingers through his hair in frustration. "All right. You win. I'll go this far. We'll make sure Mary and his little boys are taken care of while Parker rights himself. We can dip into the profits from the Marshville operation and we'll squeak by on what we're bringing in up here. But Parker has to go."

Sarah took a new tact. "How do you know he's drunk again?"

"I could smell it on his breath this evening when he came back from his delivery up to Patterson's. Made up some ridiculous story about hitting a rut and getting thrown. Cut his lip bad, he said, and used the alcohol to clean it out and numb the pain from the accident. Typical story from a boozehead. They learn to be good liars."

"And the money?"

"Said he lost it when the wagon tipped over on him."

"Maybe he's telling the truth."

James was losing his patience over the matter. "Why don't you accept the fact that he's a natural-born liar if ever there was one?" James growled. "Have you forgotten the other times? He always had some story to cover up what it was he was doing. He's lied about everything before. Why should I believe him now?"

There was a knock at the door, small and faint, but urgent. Sarah got up to answer.

"I'm bone-tired tonight, Sarah. Whoever it is, see if they can come back tomorrow." James supposed it was a neighbor who needed something or other from the store. Happened all the time. James and Sarah were gracious about it and served their customers even after hours. That was just part of setting up in a new town and being good neighbors.

Sarah opened the front door and was greeted with a blast of frigid winter wind. Snow swirled on the front porch and around her ankles and legs.

"Mrs. Williams, Mama needs your help!" The plaintive plea came from little seven-year-old Billy Thompson. He crossed his arms and hopped from one foot to the other as he shivered in the cold.

"Come in, Billy, come in." The boy stepped quickly into the warm house. "Now tell me what's wrong."

"My Mama said to come over here," he explained. "She'd have come herself only she had to take care of Eddie who's sick." Billy's baby brother was just past his first birthday. He had a deep chest cough and a fever. "Anyways, I told her I was big enough to come here all by myself."

Sarah smiled at the young lad's bravery. "Of course you are. Now what can I get for your mother? Does she need something for your brother's cough or something from the store? We'll get whatever she needs. I'm happy to help. What does she need?" James appeared at Sarah's elbow at stared stone-faced at the boy, assessing the situation.

It was then that Billy's bravery began to break down. His lip quivered and his little voice caught in his throat as he spoke. "She wants me to ask if Mr. Williams knows where my Daddy is. He didn't come home tonight and my Mama is worried."

James snorted and was about to say something that involved the words "drunken" and "bum" and "not surprised." But Sarah pinched his arm just in time and he kept quiet.

"Have you seen him, Mr. Williams? Do you know where he is?"

"Now, Billy, I'm sure everything is all right. You tell your mother I saw your daddy not more than an hour and a half ago. I'm sure he ..." James stumbled, not knowing exactly what to say the small child. "I'm sure he just had a few errands to take care of and will be home soon."

Billy looked anxious. "I don't know. He's never done this before. What with it being' so cold out tonight and all, Mama's real worried."

James marveled at the boy's allegiance. Of course his father had "done this" before. More than once.

"Tell you what, Billy," Sarah chimed, trying to be cheerful, "why don't you come on in and have a cup of warm milk and a piece of Sarah's Chocolate Candy." The boy's eyes widened at the appealing offer. "Mr. Williams will go see your mother and tell her everything is just fine. Come on into the kitchen now, honey."

Billy started to follow, but stopped. "No, I can't. It wouldn't be right," he decided. "I can't take no candy when my two little brothers don't get none. 'Sides, I gotta get back and make sure Mama's all right and see if Daddy's home."

"Oh, go on, boy," James prodded, "just go on into the kitchen. I'll check on your Mama and then find your daddy. Mrs. Williams will put some chocolates in a bag and you can share with your brothers and mother and father, plenty for everybody. A treat for the whole family! What would they think of you then?"

Billy seemed satisfied that his gentlemanly obligations would be met with that arrangement. Sarah smiled and reached out her hand. "It's okay, Billy. Come in here with me." The boy didn't need to be asked again and disappeared with Sarah through the large archway built by James that framed the kitchen.

James pulled his soggy boots back on and put on his coat and hat. "I'll be back soon," he called out to Sarah, and then stepped out into the night.

The snow was falling harder now, piling up quickly. James drew his scarf tighter around his neck and then trudged the few hundred yards to the Thompson's small log house, cursing Parker all the way. He banged on the front door loudly before he remembered the small children who might be in bed. Too late, he thought. Mary Thompson quickly opened and invited him in. She looked tired and distraught.

"I'm sorry, Mary. I hope I didn't wake the children."

"No. No. They've been asleep for a little while, now. Thank goodness you've come, Mr. Williams."

James hated to be called "Mr. Williams" but he said nothing. He knew that because he was her husband's boss, she would always be deferential no matter how many times he tried to get her to just call him James.

"Parker ain't home yet." Even though James had stepped inside, Mary still held the door open. Peering into the snowy darkness she asked, "Where's Billy?"

"Oh, he's fine. He's back at the house with Sarah. He looked cold and a little frightened, so she's letting him warm up there."

"Much obliged." Mary's shoulders drooped with relief. "You and Sarah have been such good friends to this family ever since you moved here. Givin' Parker a steady job and all. He hasn't come home yet, which just ain't like him. I'm worried something terrible happened. Have you seen him?"

James was surprised to hear Mary say this wasn't like Parker. Billy said the same thing, but a little boy's memory was not likely to be long. From what he knew, the derelict probably didn't come home a lot when he was supposed to. From what folks around White Lake had told him and from what he'd seen in the couple of years he knew him, Parker often drank away most of his money and the rest he'd gamble with, trying to make back what he'd lost in drink. Not the picture of a decent, honest family man that Mary was seeming to portray.

"I saw him about two hours ago. He ran a delivery for me up to Patterson's—up Mountain View way."

Mary's hopeful face fell. "Oh, no," she whispered, dreading the truth. "Was he ... well, you know ... had he been drinking again?"

James nodded somberly.

Mary slumped into the nearest chair, dejected. "I thought he was through with that for good. He's done good for such a long time."

James felt anger and confusion mix together in volatile anguish in his breast. Mary was a decent woman from a poor, but good, family. She and the boys deserved better, so much more than what Parker Thompson afforded them. He hated the man who would cause such grief to his own flesh and blood. But Mary said he'd stayed dry for a long period. "When was the last time? That he … uh … went off on a binge like this?" James hoped he had not been too indelicate.

"Let me think." Mary rubbed her forehead. "It has been almost a year. Yes, just around New Year's. He got drunk and was gone for two days out at his uncle's ranch."

James remembered that occasion. Parker didn't report to work at the store, so he ended up making emergency deliveries through the snow himself. James had threatened to fire Parker then, but as usual Sarah persuaded to give Mary's husband another chance. Not this time, though. His mind was set on that particular detail. "That was the last time?"

"He kept his promise, Mr. Williams. He's been home every night since then. Until tonight. I just know something's gone wrong."

James gazed upon the pitiful woman. She was deceived, blinded by her love, he concluded. He couldn't believe that a year ago was the last time Parker had this trouble. He hadn't really paid that much attention, but it seemed he had memories of Parker taking his pay in the morning and running up to Mountain View. Maybe Mary was unaware of these times. "Well, I'm sure he'll come in soon," he finally said. "Don't worry. Say, why doesn't Billy spend the night at our place? My boys will love to have him. Sarah will be delighted and we've got plenty of room. Then we'll just bring him over in the morning. How does that sound?"

Mary was appreciative. "Yes. That would be nice. The boy sure don't need to see his father come home in … in that condition." With weary apprehension she asked, "What if Parker don't come home? What if something really did, you know, happen to him?"

"Now, don't you worry about that. He'll be fine." Those were the words James said. What he thought was, "You should be glad to be rid of that tramp." What did she see in him anyway? As a man, it went against his nature to see any woman so distressed and burdened because of her husband. Any man who purposely caused his wife this kind of pain should be publicly … James found himself checking his anger once more. "I'm sure he'll be along any minute now. But I tell you what. I've got a few chores to wrap up tonight. Before Sarah and I turn in, I'll stop by again to make sure everything's all right. Does that sound okay?"

Mary stood up, a smile of relief on her face. "Thank you. You and Sarah are the best friends a soul could have."

James was uncomfortable with the praise. "If only she knew", he thought. He headed toward the door. As he reached it, Mary grabbed his hand in gratitude.

'Thank you, Mr. Williams. He is a good man, you know. He doesn't always see it in himself and that doubt keeps this weakness barking at him like a mean old barnyard dog. But you and Sarah see it. I can see it. He's a good man."

When James returned to the Thompson home it was past nine in the evening. Parker, of course, had not come home. James went to a few nearby friends and got up a search party. Niles Jensen, the sheriff, was one of them. He got two of his volunteer deputies, Elzo Thayer who ran the bank, and Jack Dayton, a postman. They didn't like being pulled from their beds, especially for Parker Thompson, but like James, they felt sorry for Mary and the kids. Besides, there was an unspoken law in these parts that you looked after each other, no matter what. Because the day would very likely come that you would need a helping hand yourself.

So the quartet of searchers mounted their horses and, with lanterns blazing, headed out toward Mountain View—the place they knew Parker Thompson would probably be. The snow was falling steadily.

"He's a good man." Mary's words kept rolling through James mind like the tide lapping relentlessly at the lake's shore. "He's a good man." James wondered how a good man could arrive at such a state. Oh, he had some idea about the strong pull of the bottle. He also heard strong men tell of the powerful hold gambling could take on a soul. The illusion of making a fast buck for nothing always pulled at foolish men's hearts, drawing them like moths to a flame. But what pointed a man to drink or play games of chance in the first place?

The party rode on silently and their horses plod along the highway to Mountain View. The snow was still falling, though not so heavy now.

Was it laziness that led men to the destructive traps Parker had fallen into? James knew Parker was generally a hard-worker. He was not an idler and would not take charity from anyone.

Was it a weak sense of responsibility to home and family? Mary said Parker was at home every night with his family. He'd kept that record for almost a year. His boy Billy obviously cared for him very much and there was no doubt that his wife loved him and he supposed that, in his way, he loved her.

Maybe it was some sort of manly challenge, the idea of beating the odds while playing loose and living free. But Parker, James observed, had never adopted the lifestyle of the irresponsible. He worked. He had a home. He was married with children. He didn't carouse with other women.

How about cowardice? James was well acquainted with fear. He soberly recalled that one day in his life years ago when he gave in to his own cowardly feelings. It still brought a sense of shame to remember it. That evening in Marshville when their beautiful twins were born and his fear sent him drinking for one lousy night. Sarah had forgiven him and had never even mentioned it again. The boys were the joy and light of his life, full of energy and laughter, and he did his best to be the kind of father they and their brothers and sister deserved. He had never touched a drop of alcohol since. Yet he still secretly felt ashamed of what his fear had led him to do that one night. Sarah had said the same thing to him as Mary said about Parker: "You're a good man, James," she said. Her belief in him had made all the difference.

"He's a good man." He couldn't get the words out of his mind. He felt a new urgency about the task of finding Parker Thompson, Mary's husband and Billy's father. "Come on boys, let's hurry it up a little," James called to his riding companions.

Less than an hour later, they found Parker Thompson's horse, the glow from the lanterns reflecting a yellow shimmer from its snow-frosted coat. Nearby lay the overturned Williams General Mercantile wagon he had taken for the deliveries earlier. Maybe he did have that accident this afternoon after all, James thought. They were still almost three miles from Mountain View. The men dismounted, tied their own animals to trees and began searching.

"Parker! Parker Thompson!" they shouted out loudly one after the other. "Call out if you can hear us!"

There was nothing but the sound of falling snow. It came down lightly now, almost stopped. They spread out in ever-widening circles, careful to stay in sight of the light from each other's lanterns. There seemed little reason to be hopeful. They expected the worst.

Fifteen minutes. Twenty. Looking was hard work in all the snow. Half an hour and still nothing.

"Hey! Over here!" It was Sheriff Jensen. "I think I've got something here!"

The rest of the search party quickly gathered around. "Looks like someone's been digging around here. Not too long ago. Scraped the snow off the ground. See?"

The combined light of the four lanterns revealed a circle cleared of snow about six feet in diameter. It seemed odd to everyone but James. He had a sinking feeling that Parker had come back to this spot because of their meeting this afternoon when he called him a drunk and a gambler. James stared at the evidence at the tip of his boots. He now confronted the likelihood that Parker had been telling the truth about the accident..

"Parker!" James screamed out to the darkness. "Parker, can you hear me? Where are you, man?"

The others felt the intensity of James' renewed calls and shouted all the more loudly. Finally, a small, pitiful noise could be heard by the men, almost like the helpless bleating of a lamb. They could not understand at first. Then they could make it out. "Here! I'm here. Oh, help me before I die!" The weak, muffled voice of Parker Thompson came from … well, no one could tell exactly where it came from.

"Hurry, boys," the sheriff urged. "He's got to be here somewhere."

"Parker!" James shouted. "Keep talking so we can get a fix on you. We're here, man. Parker!"

Finally they located a mound of snow under a stand of large trees. Parker, knowing he was in extreme difficulty, had tried to fashion a snow cave. Exhausted, he crawled in, intending to wait out the storm, either to die or return in the morning.

The rescue team dug him out. He was groggy, only partly aware of what was going on. His breath stank and an empty whiskey bottle lay beside him. "Sure am glad you boys came along," he slurred. "I'm gettin' a might cold."

"Parker, ya' dang fool, what in blazes are you doin' out here?" Niles chastised as he pulled him to his feet. "You could freeze to death tonight!"

"I know. I'm so sorry," Parker mumbled to no one in particular. His face was blue and the team rapidly built a small fire at which Parker warmed himself while the others massaged his skin to get the circulation going.

"Parker," Jack Dayton said, "you shouldn't have come out here in this storm on your own. You know better than that. A storm like this will slow up a man's blood until it won't pump anymore. What's wrong with you!"

"That's why I brought along my hot sauce," Parker replied, referring to his whiskey. He stood up from the fire and tried a step on his own, but staggered forward into Elzo Thayer's arms.

"Drunk again!" Elzo said in disgust.

"Me, too!" Parker chortled, still groggy. "But I wouldn't have had none, except to stay warm." As he looked around the circle of men, he suddenly recognized his employer. "James? James Williams? Is that you?"

"I'm here, Parker," James softly replied, drawing close to his friend and taking him by an arm. "Come on. Let's get you home. Mary's worried sick about you." The group headed back toward their horses.

Parker began to cry, blubbering out his explanation to his boss. "I'm sorry, Mr. Williams. I'm so obliged to you all for saving my life. I'm a no good fool!" He sobbed loudly and sniffed. "After my accident, I knew you was going to be mad, Mr. Williams, and when I saw you, you said I was drunk and gambled the forty dollars and I thought you was going to fire me and having to tell Mary and the boys I had no more work again …"

"Enough to drive a man to drink, eh, Parker," the sheriff said sarcastically. James frowned.

"You really did have an accident yesterday, didn't you?" James said evenly to Parker.

"Yes, sir. Just like I told you. I swear it's the God-honest truth!" He tried to hold his right arm to the square, but the liquor got the better of him and he swayed backward before being caught by James and Jack.

"I didn't believe you," James said apologetically.

Parker mumbled something nobody could understand. The he said, "So's to prove it and clear my name with you, I just had to come back, don't you see. I had to find them gold pieces and prove I can do the job." Parker started sobbing again. "You ain't gonna fire me, are you Mr. Williams? Mary couldn't stand it if I lost another job." Then he remembered something and fumbled around in his pocket for a minute. He pulled out two twenty dollar gold pieces and held them in his open, shivering palm. "There you go, sir. There's them gold pieces I was tellin' you about today. I found 'em. Right where I had the accident. I had to come back. Had to. Can't nobody say Parker Thompson ain't good to his word."

Good, indeed, James thought. He rubbed the gold pieces in his fingers, astonished at how wrong he had been about his employee, suddenly grateful he did not earlier get around to firing the man. He felt sorry and ashamed he did not believe him earlier. It would have saved all the trouble, all the grief. "Parker, you are worth a sight more than forty dollars. You could have died out here. Would have, too, if Mary hadn't sent us out."

"Then I would've died savin' the honor of my family and my name. I shoulda told Mary, though. I'm sorry for that." Parker had an air of reflectiveness about him. "I've done some evil in my day," he confessed. "I learnt that when the devil comes a knockin' you gotta either let him in or keep him out."

James and the others looked with curious, new appreciation at the man they realized they might have misjudged. Parker seemed not to notice and continued speaking.

"I learnt to overcome bad gamblin' and I take care of my family now—thanks to Mr. Williams here givin' me a job at the Mercantile, and I don't drink no more unless I have to. But the biggest thing I learnt was there are some things bigger'n death. Honorin' my word is one of 'em. So, you see, I had to come back and find them gold pieces. Or die tryin. I just had to come back and try…" He started crying and blubbering again, the effect of the whiskey.

As they arrived at the place the horses were tied up, Parker saw the broken wagon in the dim glow of the lanterns and stumbled again. Again, James and Jack caught his arms on either side and held him up. This time, it was not so roughly. This time, they held him up with respect.

Parker broke down some more. "I ain't never gonna touch another drop, Mr. Williams. I swear it. You saved my life and I'll do anything you want. Anything at all. Only, you ain't gonna fire me are you?"

James helped his friend mount up. 'Let's just get you home to Mary. She'll be so glad to see you."

"She's a good woman," Parker affirmed.

Yes, thought James. And you're a good man.

Ↄ

Wednesday, April 17.

Sarah told me an important secret to her marriage today: Remember who you are and miracles will happen.

We talked about being children of God, everyone of us. That's part of who we are.

Another part is the roots we all have in our family heritage. Sarah's book showed me that who I am has grown from the heap of ancestry, men and women who have lived and struggled, loved and died. The legacy of their efforts has given me so much. What I do with that heritage is the legacy I will leave my descendants.

She also said remembering who we are is to remember that no matter how hard it is, we should remember everyone is a brother or sister. We are all brothers and sisters on this planet. In God's eyes we are each his child and He loves everyone perfectly. That means He loves the person who disgusts me as well as he loves me. So, remembering who we are means we are supposed to serve others no matter what we think about them.

I think that's when the miracles she talks about really happen. She told me about Parker Thompson. That was William Thompson's father and Ben Thompson's grandfather. He was no good in everyone's eyes. But a miracle happened. He changed. He kept his promise. He never touched liquor again. He became a partner in James' and Sarah's store and his family still runs it. He and his wife had another son and three daughters. They turned out to be a great family here in White Lake and throughout the valley.

I'm sure that the commitment Ben Thompson mentioned to Edward has something to do with what happened to his grandfather that night. I'm not sure exactly what it is. I just know it will all work out all right.

Remember who you are and miracles will happen. That is the third secret.

I'm still feeling nauseous. I'm going to see the doctor tomorrow.

Chapter Five

You can't be home until you're home.

Corinne telephoned Ed at work late in the morning. "Let's have lunch together," she coaxed.

"It's a really busy day, hon'," he started to say, but, vaguely aware he had been losing points since roughly the start of their marriage, he meekly finished, "Well, okay. Wonderful idea. Shall I pick you up at noon? We can go to Simpson's."

"Sounds splendid!" she chirped cheerfully. "See you then!"

Corinne spent a long time on her hair. She wanted to look especially nice. The warmer spring air and brighter sunlight were blessings not to be ignored. She felt good. She had things to look forward to. She was at once excited, nervous and happy. She wanted to share all of it with Ed, to have him step into this bubbling pool of bliss with her.

With her hair done, she carefully selected just the right dress. She tried on several, of course, methodically evaluating the impact each might have on the occasion. Finally, she had it narrowed down to the small-print flower pattern with the puffy shoulders or a bright, more traditionally styled outfit made from attractive gingham. She opted for the flowers. It's more fitting for this time of year, she reasoned.

Less problematic was what shoes to wear. She only had two pairs. One of them she worked in; the other was the pair she wore when going out into public. They weren't perfect, but matched closely enough. Besides, there wasn't much choice, and it wasn't like White Lake was the fashion center of the nation. She had a birthday coming up soon and she decided some new shoes would be the perfect gift from a loving husband. That and a new dress.

Simpson's Diner was a favorite spot of theirs. When they were dating, Ed and Corinne would often end up at the place for a late night meal or some dessert. Simpson's was the unofficial gathering spot in White Lake. At first that was because there weren't any real competitors around. As the town grew, other restaurants appeared in different areas around town, but Simpson's held the advantage of being the first and oldest. Folks thought of it as "their place." So people still frequented Simpson's, from nighttime teens giddy with hormone-driven excitement, to middle-of-the-day old men congregating to grouse about the state of the union. It was where many a young man of White Lake popped the question to potential young brides. Corinne had heard Ed's proposal for marriage in Simpson's almost one year ago. In their special booth, along the middle of the west wall. Corinne hoped they might be seated in that same booth today. It would make things perfect, she concluded, for what she had to say to Ed.

Their house was just a block from Ed's office, but today he would drive to pick up his wife, park the car again at the office, and then together they would walk the short sidewalk to lunch. He checked his watch. Only 10:58. Plenty of time to do more work on the draft.

He had been given the assignment by Mr. Perkins to write out a new proposal for a financial broker from somewhere back east. With the small but persistent undercurrent of opposition to the project from Martin's Garage and Williams General, local financing efforts had been shackled. As a contingency, Tom Perkins made contact with some people he knew in Chicago who, in turn, put him touch with Richard Riceland, reputedly a financial wizard. Riceland had made his fortune in capitalizing start-up ventures like their own motor inn cabins idea. To Ed, he sounded like a savvy businessman whose shrewd eye for new business success stories was magical. It was exciting that their own project caught his attention.

There were some preliminary discussions and a sudden trip by Mr. Perkins to Chicago, where he would meet the gentleman who held the key to the future of the cabins. The interest in working together was strong enough on both sides that even before the long train ride home, Mr. Perkins had telephoned Ed and asked him to start drafting a new business plan.

It was exhilarating to Ed, young as he was, to be trusted with significant tasks important to bringing to pass a wonderful vision. He was ambitious and worked hard, watching and learning, eagerly throwing himself into the tasks that Mr. Perkins threw his way. Today, he wrote. When he next glanced at his watch it read 11:59.

"Holy smoke! Look at the time!" he exclaimed aloud, jumping up from his seat. He dropped his pencil on his desk, grabbed his hat and coat and rushed out the door. He called to the receptionist on his way out, "I'm taking Corinne to lunch, Myrtle. Be back in about an hour!"

Myrtle tried to respond, but Ed was gone.

He arrived four minutes late. Corinne tried to bite her tongue, but she couldn't help herself. "You're late," she hissed.

"I know. I'm sorry, dear, but I got involved with work and time just got away a little bit. I got here as soon as I could. It's only five minutes."

"Those are five minutes that tell me what's most important to you, Ed Whitmore," Corinne snipped, "and it's obviously not me!"

Ed hated being put on the defensive. "Okay. Okay. I said I was sorry. I'm sorry. Let's just go, shall we?"

"You don't seem very sorry to me," Corinne persisted. "You haven't even said anything about how I look."

"Perhaps that has something to do with the fact that I just now arrived and have had to spend my time defending myself for being slightly late," Ed frowned. "You know, if you don't want to go, I do have a lot of work I should get back to."

Corinne struggled to control herself. This wasn't the way it was supposed to be. She didn't know why she let little things like this upset her, but lately it seemed every tiny annoyance opened a dam releasing a flood of unusually intense emotion. She had never been like this before. She didn't understand it, so she realized she couldn't expect Ed to understand it either. "I'm sorry, dear," she humbly offered. "You are right. Let's just go and have a nice time, shall we?" Before he could argue, she took him by the arm and let him lead her out the front door to the car.

Ed relaxed and brightened, now actually eager to have a lunch date with his wife. He opened her car door for her and said, "You look beautiful, hon."

She smiled, gave him a quick hug, and stepped into the car.

Simpson's had an average crowd and Corinne was pleased that Ed took her suggestion to request their special booth. Their hostess, Patty Roper, was a long-time friend of Ed's parents and was only too happy to oblige. "No problem at all, Eddie. You two kids need the privacy," she loudly said when he asked.

Ed flushed with embarrassment because a man doing important things in this world shouldn't be called by his childhood moniker, and doubly so because when she said "need the privacy," heads turned and eyes stared and knowing smiles blossomed from every other customer in the room. He hurriedly ushered Corinne to her place and then sat down across from her.

Although it hadn't changed in years, each of them carefully pored over the dog-eared menus as if to discover some new tantalizing dish. It was a foregone conclusion that Ed would order what he always ordered (fresh trout and vegetables) and Corinne would order what she always ordered (the roast beef plate). Still they discussed tempting options.

"The mashed potatoes and fried chicken looks good, doesn't it?"

"Hmmm. Yes, it really does. Are you going to order it?"

"I don't know. The roast beef plate is *so* delicious. It's hard to pass up a chance at that."

"I know what you mean. I think I'll get the trout today. But the meat pie might be good, too."

After several minutes of this sort of chatter, Patty appeared and cheerfully took their orders—Ed going for the trout and vegetables, and Corinne ordering the roast beef plate.

Today, however, they splurged on a chocolate malt, which they would share. Daring.

"This is nice," Ed said, once they were served. "We should do it more often."

"That would be nice," Corinne agreed. "It would be like when we were dating."

"Sorry about being late, hon," Ed apologized again. This time he felt more sincere about it. "Mr. Perkins gets back from Chicago tomorrow. You know, the contact for financial backing I told you about before? Anyway, I have to have that new business plan draft ready for him when he gets here. I was working on that and just lost track of the time. I'm really sorry."

"Apology accepted. I'm sorry I snapped at you."

"No, I deserved it. Look, let's just have a leisurely lunch. No time worry, no pressures. I'll get back to the office when I get back. I'd rather spend the time with you anyway."

"That's sweet. Thank you."

"You're dressed nicely today. Some special occasion I forgot?" One of Ed's recurring fears was that he would inadvertently upset Corinne by forgetting one of the myriad of "anniversaries" she attached meaning to. Maybe today was the day two years ago that they first came to Simpson's on a date. Or maybe it was the anniversary of the first time he saw her in the dress she was wearing or the first time she rode in the car with him or … She was sentimentally romantic that way, with an incredible mind for remembering those kinds of events. Ed never remembered things like that. It wasn't that he didn't want to—he saw how disappointed she was that he didn't remember—it was just that, try as he might, he simply couldn't.

"Thank you for the compliment," Corinne responded, pleased at her husband's effort. She didn't want to tell him yet. The timing didn't feel right to her. So she changed the subject. "I thought you wrote a business plan before. Can't you just use that one for Mr. Perkins' contact?"

Ed smiled. "No, no, dear. That wouldn't do. You see, Mr. Perkins thinks he has found some financing from back East. That means we won't have to wait on approval from the bank here and they're still holding things up because of Willie Martin and Ben Thompson. If all goes well, in a couple of months we should have our package together and can begin construction. We could get a lot done before the winter snows catch us."

"So why do you have to have another plan? You worked so hard on the last one. The bank was quite impressed. Why not just use that one?"

Ed chuckled. "My pretty little wife ..."

Corinne grit her teeth. She loathed the condescending attitude that Ed sometimes lapsed into when he spoke about business matters with her. He was getting better about showing her respect, but when he felt pressured he would assume an air of superiority.

She knew it was all bravado to cover up his own insecurity and inexperience, but she wished he would speak to her as an intellectual equal. She took seriously the challenge to study and be interested in all sorts of matters, including business affairs.

"That's just the way their world works," Ed continued. "These people Mr. Perkins has been dealing with are just a whole lot more sophisticated. We can't come off sounding like we're small town ignoramuses. We're moving into a whole new sphere now, and our plans need to reflect our ambitions."

"Sounds exciting. But, honestly Edward, compared to Chicago and New York, isn't White Lake 'small town'? Don't think you can hide that fact, do you?"

"Well, no, not that part," Ed conceded. "But that doesn't mean we have to think small. It took big men with big vision to make a Chicago or a New York. It took determination and money and energy."

"And people," Corinne reminded.

"Yes, well, you're right about one thing. It is all very exciting. I'm excited. So is Mr. Perkins. He goes on about how he is amazed at our good luck, but I don't think it's luck at all. I think it's a real blessing. That's what it is. It's a blessing that comes from the greatness and vitality of the country we live in. It flows from the determination and creativity of people who are willing to lay it on the line to realize big dreams."

"You're so talented and smart, dear," Corinne said sincerely. "You're such a good husband and a splendid businessman. I'm sure you will impress Mr. Perkins' contact. By the way, who is it?"

"A man who is actually quite well-known in financial circles. Considered a genius, very wealthy, from out of Boston and New York. Richard Riceland is his name."

Corinne arched her eyebrows in skeptical curiosity. "Richard Riceland. Richard Riceland. Hmm. Where have I heard that name before?"

Ed smiled thinly. "I doubt you've heard of him, hon, unless you follow business finance. A little out of your realm, I think. Even I'm not all that familiar with him, just what Mr. Perkins and a few others have told me."

"I'm sure I've come across that name. Richard Riceland." Corinne brightened. "I know where it was! Just by chance, I read an article about a financier from back east in the *Wall Street Journal* over at the library about a month ago. You know I go there once a week to read, right?" she asked pointedly.

"Uh, yeah, that's right. I guess I knew you did. Didn't know you read business periodicals, though."

"Anyway, amidst the stock and other market reports was this article about a Richard Riceland, a real wealthy guy. I can't remember where he was from, but it could have been the Boston area. It called him 'The Raider,' because it's a name some of his associates came up with. Seems like he makes his fortune off the misfortune of others."

"How so?" It was Ed's turn to be curious.

"If I remember correctly, he backs start-up enterprises on very liberal terms. But when they begin to fail—which the majority of the businesses he backs do—the owners are forced to give up all their assets to him. He then turns around and carves up those assets, selling them at bargain basement prices. He invests pennies and ruthlessly squeezes out dollars. The owners end up broke, he ends up rich. That's why they call him 'The Raider'. I guess a lot of businessmen think he's just a good, hard-nosed dealer and admire him for the wealth he's accumulated."

Ed was stunned. "I didn't know you read the *WSJ*."

There are a lot of things you don't know about me, she thought. She was determined to keep the conversation upbeat.

"Sometimes I enjoy reading it," Corinne admitted. "I do try to stay abreast of a lot of things, though, and I happened to see this about a Richard Riceland. I'm sure that was the name."

"What edition? Can you remember that?"

"Sorry. It was about a month ago, I think."

Ed shook his head in disbelief. "Can't be the same fellow. Mr. Perkins is a smart businessman and he would know about this, I'm sure. He's very careful and conservative, you know, not like some of these wild speculators you hear about in the stock market these days. Of course, some are smart about it. This Richard Riceland has built up millions in the stock market. Blue chip stuff mostly. The market's really been going great guns for a long time now."

"I know it has. Can't last forever."

"Anyway, I'm sure it's not the same fellow. Even if it was, our project is not going to fail."

"How can you be so sure, Ed? I mean, you haven't even bought the land from the Nates yet."

"It's a fool proof plan! At least, if I ever get the plan written it will be." Ed said this last bit looking at his watch, signaling he was eager to leave. The conversation built up his nervous energy and he wanted to throw himself into the tasks of the project at hand.

"Ed," Corinne pleaded earnestly, reaching across the booth and catching his arm, "just be very careful about what you get us into, will you?"

The intensity of his wife's plea impressed Ed. "Of course I will, darling. It will work out spectacularly well. You'll see."

"I have a bad feeling about this Riceland fellow. Promise me not to get our resources tangled up with him."

"I'm sure …"

"Ed," Corinne interrupted, "just promise me."

"Okay, I promise."

Corinne let go of his arm, but still spoke intently. "I just think we can't do anything that will jeopardize our security right now. We absolutely can't."

"I won't. I promise." Ed was puzzled. In the past, his wife and he had talked about taking calculated risks in order to get ahead. She was enthusiastic and supportive then. He reminded her, "But even if the cabins don't become profitable, we can always start again. You know, we're young and free. We can do anything we'd like."

"Not anymore," Corinne quietly replied.

"What do you mean? Of course we can. That's the greatness of this country. Why not?"

"It's the reason I wanted to have lunch with you. I went to Dr. Moore's office this morning and he confirmed it. Ed, we're going to have a baby!"

CB

The next day, Corinne relished the telling of the experience to Sarah Williams. "He was simply shocked, Sarah. Flabbergasted. I think he had no idea that I might be pregnant, and when he found out, he didn't know how to act or what to say. It was so cute. He became very protective of me. He actually asked if I would be all right, if he needed to take me home so I could get some rest, or if I should be taking some other precaution."

Sarah nodded with understanding. "Mmm, hmm. Just like James."

"When we walked back to the car, and then again when we got home, he held my arm and walked slowly, like he thought I was going to fall and shatter like crystal or something. He was so sweet!"

Sarah smiled. "Men. God bless them. My boys and daughter's husbands were the same way. Maybe they have a club where they go when their wives become pregnant to learn these things."

"I know. It's pretty funny. They act totally helpless."

"It's understandable though, don't you think?" Sarah asked her young friend. "They will never know, like we do, what it is to so intimately share God's power to create life. Think of it! There is a gift of intelligence that only we, as women, have. It gives us the capacity to grow cells and organs and hair and nails and feet and arms. It's an amazing blessing, a light kindled by our husbands, but held exclusively by us. Ed will never feel the special changes that take place inside you as a new little person forms and grows. And I don't mean just the physical changes, but emotional and spiritual, too. He will never experience giving birth or the incredible power of the bond of motherhood. So he will do the best he can with what he sees and feels. Our men fuss over us, perform wonderfully sweet, if sometimes pitifully irrelevant, solicitations to 'make things easier' for us. But in reality they can only stand on the sidelines and watch as we get to directly participate in a wondrous miracle."

Corinne was thoughtfully quiet. "I hadn't thought of it that way," she admitted. She brightened. "Ed was so cute. Now that I think about it, maybe part of his shock might be the idea of another mouth to feed scares him. He's very responsible that way."

Sarah nodded and reached for Corinne's hand, which she clasped between her own wrinkled palms, one on top and one underneath. "Ed is a good boy. You've done well by him, dear. When the baby's come, he'll be able to be more involved in his role as father then. He'll figure it out, I'm sure."

"I'm going to have a baby!" Corinne beamed. "Ed's going to be a father! And my mother's going to be a grandmother!" It all seemed surreal to her at the moment, like she was reliving the little girl dreams long ago tucked away in her heart, the fantasy of marrying Prince Charming and of having a family and of living happily ever after.

Corinne arose, the warm sense of well being swelling in her bosom. She walked into the kitchen where earlier she put a large pan of water to warm on the stove. How contented she was! Whatever shadows of confusion lingered about being happy in her marriage with Ed fled now in the sunshine of her new status: she was going to be a mother. She was going to have a baby!

She poured the pan of warm water into a large foot basin and tested the temperature. Too hot. She added cool water until it was just right and then toted the heavy bowl back into the sitting room where the bare-footed Sarah waited expectantly.

"Oh, my, this is wonderful. Thank you, dear," the old woman sighed as she placed both feet in the inviting bath to soak. The soak was part of the ritual now, followed by a brisk rubdown with a towel, then the trimming of nails made more pliant by the water, and finally a foot massage.

"You are most welcome."

Corinne genuinely enjoyed this little service now. She thought how different it was from that first day more than four months ago when she reluctantly—and amateurishly—carved away on Sarah's toenails. How much she had learned! About toenails, about Sarah and James, about life, about herself.

"Now, dear, tell me again. When is the baby due?"

"Dr. Moore thinks around the end of the year or the first of the new year."

"Oh, oh. Could be a Christmas surprise in the Whitmore household this year," Sarah teased. "Perfect, isn't it? Considering that the reason for Christmas began with a baby, I mean."

"Same time of year your first were born, wasn't it?"

"Not quite, dear. Jimmy and Chris were born October 16th. But yours is marvelous. Makes celebrating the holidays even more special, I'd say. I'm very happy for you and your husband, dear."

"Oh, thank you. It's just so … so … exciting!"

Sarah lifted her feet from the basin and Corinne dried them with a plush towel. She took the nail nippers and began with Sarah's right foot.

Ↄ

From the start, Sarah could tell her twins were unusual. Not because they were hers, but they *were* unusual boys. No one ever saw Jimmy and Chris apart, even as babies. When one got hungry, the other decided he was hungry, too. When one wanted to sleep, the other would go lay down beside his brother and they would nap together. They played together, they worked together, they laughed and sang together. The older they got, the closer they grew.

Sarah dearly loved her boys. But their dad … well, their dad was especially fond of them. For the first two or three years when he was tormented with his guilt about what he'd done while they were being born, he wouldn't have anything to do with them. After he squared that with his wife, though, he absolutely adored their twins. They had a kind of magical bond between them. When they were little guys, no older than six or seven years, he took them with him to make the annual candy deliveries at Christmas time in White Lake. It was the first year after they moved up from Marshville and James was splitting time between the two stores. When it was time to go down there to do the deliveries, they begged to go with him.

"Boys," James gently explained, "It's a long, hard trip even for me. With me gone, I was thinkin' I could count on my two little men to watch over things here at home and help Mother make the candy and watch your baby brothers. Besides, you'll miss the Christmas party over at the church building. You wouldn't want to skip that, now would you? I hear a very special visitor is making plans to come."

"Yes, sir," Jimmy meekly said. "We were just hoping ..."

"That we could spend time with you, Daddy," Chris finished. There was a long pause as James looked upon his little sons, heads hung down in disappointment. Chris suddenly looked up and said, "Dad?"

"Yes, son."

"Don't you get a good feeling when you give the candy to the poor families?"

A lump formed in James' throat, which he struggled to swallow. He kneeled down and with his broad, strong arms, pulled his boys close to him. "Yes, son, I surely do."

"Dad?"

"Yes, son?"

"We get a good feeling, too," Chris said sincerely. "The party would be fun and all, but we would just be thinking about how happy ... "

" ... we would be with you, to help the poor boys and girls at Christmas," Jimmy finished. "It's the best Christmas present we can think of. You don't have to get us another thing at all. Only let us go with you."

James stood, wiped a little something from his eye, and cleared a choked throat. He couldn't say no. Jimmy and Chris beamed with delight. They really *were* unusual boys.

For the twins, the move from Marshville to White Lake was all just a big adventure. They couldn't understand how hard things were for people then. They simply made new friends, lived in a new house, explored a growing city where there were more things to do. Plus, they still got to see some of their old friends in Marshville when they went on those trips with James every Christmas, and sometimes in the summer, too.

James and Sarah decided early on after moving that their family was too important to play second fiddle to the stores or building a fortune or anything else in this world. James made it a point to be home as much as humanly possible. He had a saying, "You can't be home until you're home."

Some men said that it was not the amount of time but the quality of time that counted. If you asked James, that was nonsense. To him, it was all about time.

He worked long, hard hours and was very, very busy. With the railroad going through and the mines opening up in Mountain View, White Lake grew like a brush fire in a late summer wind. Naturally, so did Williams General Store, being the only place for many years where folks could buy a majority of their supplies. They were in the right place at the right time and James worked like a dog to keep up with the growth. When James took on Parker Thompson, he was a big help.

Sarah did her share, too, but with the family increasing in size, she devoted more of her time to their home and rearing the young ones. She still supervised the candy production, even after they combined that with the operations of the main store. By then, Sarah had it down to a science and she hired others to do the mixing and cooking and packaging.

Being the owners of the only general store in a fast-growing town meant that James and Sarah Williams became "important" people in the eyes of other folks who thought of themselves as being important people. James was recruited to run for City Council. Later they wanted him to go for a State Senate seat. He did his duty. He was an honest man, a good man, and very busy. But through it all, he always believed his first duty was to Sarah and the children. He always did his best to come home.

In time, other children came along. Frank and Peter were born before they moved, and Merlin and Maggie were born in White Lake. Sarah learned firsthand that having a baby changed everything. Having six was like organizing earthworms.

She tried to explain her insight to James one evening as they sat together for a quiet moment alone on their front porch. "You know, James, you still have all your chores and work to take care of. And I have mine—the cooking and washing and ironing and mending—only more of it. You have to make adjustments and plan things out. We both do. Together. Sometimes I wonder how we keep going and do what we do."

They thought about the others in White Lake and realized they weren't any different. Those folks were just as busy building a city and building lives, all while rearing their families and trying to be the best people they could be.

"Of course," Sarah continued, "it's not even the daily routine chores that change with having children, because you can adjust to that pretty quickly. With kids, though, there are a hundred little emergencies that come up. It's a scraped knee or bloody nose. It's a bruised spirit when cruel classmates taunt with vicious names. It's runny noses and chills and fever. It's a lost rabbit escaped from its hutch or missing socks. Or complaints of nothing good to eat, even though the pantry is full. Or of 'nothing to do'."

If having children changed everything, their commitment to their family did not. James and Sarah made sure they gave enough time at home, no matter how busy they became otherwise.

The twins adjusted to the fact James was a lot busier right off. They simply figured that if Dad had to go to work every day, they would get more time with him by going to where he was. So they'd meander on up from the house over to the store just so they could be with their dad.

Some men would be angry at the interruption and send their boys back home where they belonged. Others would be tolerant, allowing their sons to stay as long as they didn't get in the way. James was in that rare class of leaders who warmly welcomed his sons without apology or embarrassment. He went out of his way to find ways to let them be useful in the store. He loved working side by side with them. Customers would sometimes ask, "James, why don't you send those boys home? You could sell a whole lot more with them out of the way."

"I'm not trying to sell more," James always replied patiently. "I'm trying to rear boys." He believed that in the grand scheme of things, his highest calling and most important work was as a husband and father.

One day, when the boys were stocking the display tables that we used back then, they heard a ruckus out in front of the store.

"What is that?" Jimmy exclaimed, eyes wide with wonder.

"I dunno. It sounds like birds and thunder," Chris replied, eyes equally wide. "And like …"

"Like children playing!" Jimmy cried. They remained frozen for a fraction of an instant longer. Then, glancing briefly at each other, they simultaneously grinned, yelled, "Let's go!" and burst out the front door and into the street.

The picture that greeted them was something they'd never before seen. A small band paraded down the avenue, trumpets and horns raucously blaring, clarinets and flutes teasing with a lively melody, bass drums thundering a relentless beat. Children danced playfully behind, while their dogs raced in and out and through the marching musical mayhem. It was only the City Council's way of promoting the start of the Founder's Day celebration. But Jimmy and Chris had never heard or seen such a thing before. To them, it was pure ecstasy.

James brought them home for supper that evening. They exploded through the front door, "Mom! Mom! Guess what!"

"My goodness," said Sarah, "what on earth has gotten into you two this evening?"

"We saw this parade at the store today and they had people playing horns and drums and things," Jimmy said breathlessly.

"And they were making music, real music," Chris added with great enthusiasm.

James winked at me, a big grin on his face as the boys demonstrated by marching around the room, mimicking band sounds with their childish voices.

"And guess what?" Jimmy continued. "We're going to the gazebo at Center Park tonight."

"They're going to have more music," Chris piped in. "Me and Jimmy want to learn how to play real music, too. Dad said we could."

Sarah shot a quizzical look at her husband. "James?"

"I'll talk to you later," he said quickly. "Boys, let's wash up and help Mother with supper. Then we'll head on over to the park."

After they ate, the family walked to the opening of the Founder's Day festivities. James pushed the buggy holding little Maggie. Sarah held Merlin's hand. His short little legs meant it was a slow walk, so the twins and the other boys skipped on ahead.

"What do you think about getting the boys some instruments, Sarah?" James asked. "Wouldn't it be grand to have a family band?"

Sarah cocked her head and looked at the father of her children as if he had gone loco. The wheels of his mind were churning at full speed. His entire body glowed with enthusiasm over the inspiration that had come to him.

"Think of it. You know the piano. I can brush up on my fiddling, maybe play a little bass. The boys are old enough and certainly interested enough. I think we could get a little family band going. Wouldn't that be fun?"

"Fun. Oh, yes, fun," she replied cynically.

That was all the encouragement James needed. From then on, Williams' family recreation usually involved some sort of music they made together. Jimmy took up the fiddle and Chris was partial to the clarinet. They took to their instruments like ducks to water. Oh, they had natural talent. But they also had passion and that drove them to spend hours upon hours practicing, experimenting, inventing, playing. They made music.

The rest loved playing, too. Frank and Peter and Merlin took up drums and flute and accordion. In a year or two the family was good enough to be asked to perform a few numbers at community events. A year or two after that they played a few dances. They traveled to some of the surrounding towns to play. One Christmas they did a show down in Marshville, which they especially relished.

Jimmy and Chris were the bright lights in the family band. Music for them became more than a pastime. It was their life. Every day they spent hours upon hours playing. School was just a way to kill time before they could get back to making their music. The only one who could match their energy was James. He fiddled and played with the boys every spare moment he got. And so the twins grew even closer to each other and to their dad.

One evening the boys stayed after school to talk to their teachers about trying to get a school band going. James figured they would just go right home after they finished, so he and Sarah took the other kids and visited the new restaurant that had just opened up by Wally and Lisa Simpson, just a block from the store. They wanted to introduce themselves, get some pie. Then they, too, would head back to the house.

"Jimmy! Chris! We're home," Sarah called as they entered the front door. There was no answer.

"James, do you see the boys anywhere?"

"No, dear. Jimmy! Chris!" His voice was much louder than hers. Still no answer. James frowned. "Wonder if they've come back from their school meeting yet."

Sarah started to worry. By now she had walked through the entire house and looked in the back, but there was no sign of them. "James, I hope nothing has happened."

"I'm sure everything is fine. Probably a long meeting. I'll head on over to the school and check. Why don't you get the little ones ready for bed."

"Can't we play some music?" Frank pleaded, though he was just stalling, trying to delay his bedtime.

"Go on, Frank," I said. "Get ready for bed. Dad's going to go get Jimmy and Chris. Then maybe we'll have some time to play." The children obediently hustled off to the bedroom.

Thirty minutes later James returned without the twins and with a concerned crease in his brow. "There was no one at the school," he said, "so I went over to Julie Sprague's. She said she and the other teachers had the meeting, all right, and Jimmy and Chris were there, but that they had finished about 5:00. That was two hours ago."

"Where could they be?" Sarah asked. "Did you check the store?"

"Yep. All locked up. I went in and no one's there. Didn't look like they'd been there."

"What should we do? Shall we get Sheriff Jensen?"

James took a deep breath, but did not answer directly. He signaled with a slight nod toward the four youngsters standing in the sitting room doorway in their bedclothes, somber looks on their faces. "Did you find Jimmy and Chris?" Peter asked in a weak little voice.

"Come in here," James invited the children. They hurried in to join their parents. "Jimmy and Chris left the school about two hours ago. Now, we're sure they're all right, but we don't know where they are at this moment."

"Should we pray?" Frank asked. It was the first and best thing he could think of in a situation like this.

"Yes, Frank," Sarah replied. "Let's pray very hard."

"Good idea, Frank. Come on," James said, getting to his knees. "Let's ask Heavenly Father to help."

The scene was touching to Sarah as she watched her little ones, even four-year-old Maggie, follow their father's example by falling to their knees and folding their arms. There was power and strength in this family. They worked together, sang together, read and made music together. They taught each other the best things that they knew.

Now it was time to pray together.

"I'll start," said James, "then if any of the rest of you want to add something, you can go right ahead."

They had prayed together as a family before. God answered their prayers, they knew. They believed that God, who knows when a single sparrow falls, knew now where Jimmy and Chris were. So, the Williams family prayed to God. Only this time it seemed more than just praying. It seemed they literally talked with a loving Father.

When it was her turn, Maggie summed it best: "Please, Heavenly Father. Please bless Mommy and Daddy so they won't worry. Bless me and Frankie and Pete and Merlin and Jimmy and Chris. And please bring me back my Jimmy and Chris. They're my brothers and they're lost. They can make music, so we need them back home."

Call it coincidence, call it faith, or call it whatever you like. No sooner had they said "amen" than the twins came running through the front door, though obviously shaken and scared. Jimmy had a red spot under his eye that would darken in the next day or two. Both had scrapes and scratches on their arms. Each clutched his case containing his instrument.

"Jimmy! Chris!" Sarah ran to hug them, closely followed by James and the children.

"Where on earth have you been, boys?" James asked. "You look like you've wrestled a ghost."

"It was terrible, Dad," Jimmy explained. "After our meeting at school, we headed for home. It was just starting to get dark. We heard this noise …"

"Like someone was following us," Chris interjected.

"That's it. But we couldn't see anybody, so we just kept walking. Then these boys I've never seen before …"

"Three of them, all older than us,"

"… they jumped on us and tried to take our instruments away. They were using the most awful language and saying we were sissies, like girls, because we played music. They said the Williams were thieves who got where they were because they took property that wasn't theirs and now they were going to start makin' us pay."

"Jimmy got hit first, but he whacked one of 'em pretty good with his fiddle case. I got some good licks in, too. Enough to get 'em off so we could run back to the school."

"But no one was there," Jimmy continued. "I guess they'd all gone home after the meeting. We could hear those boys coming after us, so we snuck away as quiet as we could."

"They didn't hear us," Chris added, "but we could hear them. They said if they caught us they were going to whip us and if we told, they'd kill us. The one of 'em said to go check down at the store."

"That's where we were going until we heard that," Jimmy picked up. "So we went over to the church building and hid there."

"We figured people like that wouldn't want to be too near the church," Chris explained.

"Anyway, we waited for a while and didn't hear anything more, so we came on home going down Seventh Street, instead of Third, like we usually do."

"Thank goodness you're safe," Sarah sighed in relief.

"We prayed and then you came in," Maggie pointed out. There was no doubt in her mind that she had simply talked to

Heavenly Father and so, of course, the twins came home. That's what they asked Him to do.

After things settled down a bit, the family played one tune together—that always worked to calm their hearts. They prayed again, giving thanks for the safe return of the twins. When everyone was in bed, Sarah asked James about the boys who attacked Jimmy and Chris.

"Do you know who they are? What do they mean we 'stole property' to get what we have? We've worked long and hard to make the modest gains we've made!" She was upset that anyone accused them or doubted their integrity!

James was quiet for a long time. "I think I might have an idea," he said. "Do you remember when we bought the place the store is sitting on?"

"Yes. From old man Jackson. Paid cash down and then the rest six months later. Those were the terms."

"Right. Well, do you remember him mentioning something about an old settler who'd wanted the property first but turned down his offer? The fellow didn't have the money up front. Mr. Jackson said he didn't offer terms because he had no faith the fellow could come up with the money to pay it off. Remember?"

"Vaguely. That didn't have anything to do with us, though. We made an offer fair and square and made good on it."

"Yes, I know. But I think that old settler may be back in town. I heard rumor of it this morning in the store. I didn't think anything of it because, like you said, we did our deal all fair and square."

"Well, why do you think he's connected to this?"

"Just that I remember Mr. Jackson talking about what a bitter fellow this man was."

"So?"

"That and someone who mentioned they'd seen him in town today. Said he had his three boys with him."

"Three boys? Oh, James, do you think …?"

"Could be. I don't know for sure. Clinton. Joe Clinton's the name."

℞

Tuesday, June 4.

Ed and I are going to have a baby! We are both excited. I get hungry often these days and the cravings everyone talks about are real. I wanted sauerkraut and tons of cheese today. It's due at the end of the year. We're starting to think of names and have it narrowed down to a list of about five girls' names and six boys'. When I told Sarah today she was just as happy as we are. She is a wonderful lady.

She talked a lot about her family today, and getting started here in White Lake. She rambled a bit, I think. She may have been a little tired today. And she is getting old. Still, I love being with her and listening to her stories.

She talked about their family band that they had. It was something they all enjoyed, especially the twins. One played fiddle and the other clarinet. I wonder if the instruments in the glass case in the entryway of Sarah's house were Chris' and Jimmy's? Anyway, they kept close as a family. Sarah's rule was to "Teach goodness, work together and read, play and pray together." Sounds like a good rule to me.

James had a rule, too. When I mentioned it to Ed, he didn't really understand it, I don't think. At least, he wouldn't talk to me about it in too much depth. He's pretty absorbed in this motor inn cabins deal with Richard Riceland looking at it. I'm worried about him. All the more reason, I think, for him to think about James' rule, the fourth secret.

"You can't be home until you're home."

I hope and pray Ed comes home before he can't.

Chapter Six

If you miss the joy, you miss it all.

Corinne and Ed quarreled more. Corinne knew changes were happening, but couldn't quite figure out what it was. They still loved each other. At least, she still loved Ed, still adored his strong shoulders and his flashing, charismatic smile. His engaging, "take charge" personality was still appealing and was one of the qualities that drew her to him in the first place. And those warm, penetrating gray eyes of his could still melt her with a single stare.

Edward, on the other hand, was not as quick to understand that change was taking place in his marriage. Corinne was still the love of his life and he aimed to prove it to her. Why else would he work so hard? Why else did he lay everything on the line each and every day?

He did notice she was more easily irritated these days, but he passed that off as having something to do with her being pregnant. She seemed to need more in her condition, of that there was no doubt in his mind. He thought he pampered her—he lifted the heavier things for her, did more of the housework (even the dish washing!), and generally found little ways to be solicitous of her physical needs—but no matter how hard he tried, it never seemed to be enough. She could never get comfortable. She complained more. With pressure building at work and the Riceland deal at a critical juncture, the last thing he wanted was to manage a first-time pregnant wife making increasingly intense demands. Didn't she understand that?

They quarreled more.

Corinne knew the burden on Ed's shoulders. Their money was gone and Ed's commissions barely trickled in. She saw how it practically killed him to be making so little while big dreams burned inside him. He was counting heavily on the motor inn cabins project. If it worked according to plan, Ed assured her, they would surely become rich. Meanwhile, they were skimping by and it was taking its toll.

Living frugally was okay with Corrine as long as she knew Ed loved her. But he was so grumpy these days and irritated by the smallest things, like dinner not being on time or the mention of the lawn, which needed mowing. She concluded it must have something to do with a man's instincts to protect and provide for his family. He probably didn't feel real good about how he was doing in that arena these days. The tighter things got, the more distant he seemed. She didn't care about getting rich. She didn't care if he became important in the community. She deeply needed him to share with her in the experience of bringing their first child into the world. She just needed him to pay attention to her. Didn't he understand that?

There crept into their conversations much of the negative and less of bright dreams and optimism. There was more talk of trial and difficulty and less of the refreshing prose of love. There was more of the mundane, less of delight and happiness. They both sensed it.

They quarreled more.

The summer heat was already suffocating that morning. Corinne tugged the pull chain on the large ceiling fan that Edward installed in the kitchen just two weeks before. She tied her apron strings, noticed her growing abdomen and thought she would soon need to get a new apron, one with longer strings. She switched on the Victrola radio in their living room and returned to the kitchen to get Ed's breakfast ready.

When the machine's tubes warmed up, the mellow sound of Perry White—the silver voice of KWLK in White Lake—entered the house like a welcome guest. He was just finishing the weather report. Seventy-eight degrees, and it was only five minutes past seven. Going up to the nineties today. Just the thought made Corinne sweat with discomfort. Carrying a child definitely had its trials.

"Good morning, dear," Ed said cheerily as he came in from the bedroom, adjusting his tie.

"Good morning," Corinne pleasantly responded. "The eggs are almost done."

"Wonderful!" He crossed the kitchen floor and hugged her from behind, patting her swollen stomach. "And how's my beautiful wife this morning?" He planted an affectionate kiss on her cheek.

Corinne was pleased he asked. "I'm feeling fine. Really quite well, today, thanks for asking." She turned sausage frying in the pan. "It's going to be a hot one though. Perry White said we're headed for a heat spell. Just what I need in my condition, don't you think?"

"Hmm," Ed acknowledged, opening his newspaper as he sat down.

"Busy day today?" she asked while setting the dishes on the small table.

"Oh, fairly busy, I suppose," he replied nonchalantly without looking up from his paper. "A couple of Richard Riceland's people are coming in Thursday, you know, so we're getting ready for that."

"Oh?"

"Yeah. Bringing the papers for us to look over on the deal." Ed quickly switched topics. "Hey, the Bears beat Mountain View last night. Says here Glen Rich hit two more home runs for our boys. Four RBIs. He's fabulous, having a great year. Wouldn't surprise me at all if he ends up playing for the Yankees some day."

"Hmm," Corinne nodded.

Ed sparkled with energy. "I think we'll go all the way this year. With Glen's hitting and Ben Thompson's boy Matt on the mound, we're in great shape to make a run at the State championship. Probably Regionals, too. I'll have to give Les a call this morning."

Lester and Alice Rich were insurance customers, and Ed liked to find ways to stay close to his customers. The fact that their son was a local baseball phenomenon had Les bursting his buttons with pride. Never mind the occasional jokes around town about his name. His parents, in one of those unthinking accidents, named him after his maternal grandfather, Lester Clark, never realizing the shortened version of his given name coupled with his surname would make him an easy target of sniggering locals. Les Rich. He kept his sense of humor over the years, but now Glen was changing all that. Now he could walk about town and get respect. Without the sniggering.

Corinne served the food and Ed offered the blessing on it. They ate in silence, but Corinne was itching to hear more about the Thursday meeting with Riceland's representatives. It was in her nature to be supportive of Ed and his enthusiasm was beginning to rub off on her, sweeping her towards belief in the financing strategy. Still, in the depths of her heart, nagging fears and pestering doubts lurked. Finally, she could stand it no more and broke the quiet. "Now who are these visitors you're meeting Thursday?"

Ed finished chewing, swallowed, and dabbed at his mouth with his linen napkin. "Oh, yes. Well, they're with Richard Riceland's group. One gentleman, Carl DeWitt, is an accountant-type, a finance guy. I understand he's worked up the final numbers on the deal. The other fellow is Saul Weinstein. He's their legal beagle, you know, to make sure all the I's are dotted and T's crossed."

"You're that far along?" Corinne asked in surprise.

"Yes, we are."

"I thought you had to work out the terms of sale with the current land owners first."

"Done. Well, in principle, at least."

"Really?" Again Corinne showed surprise in her arched eyebrows. "Are the Nates really going to sell?"

"They say so."

"I hear they're in rough times right now. I know that if they sell, they need to get a lot out of it to carry them for a while. It's all they have to work with, I know that much."

The muscles in Ed's jaw tightened reflexively. "Steve Nate should have been smarter a few years ago when Tom Perkins offered to buy his land. He could have gotten twice as much for it then when he wasn't so desperate. He doesn't have much to bargain with today."

"Why, Ed Whitmore, I'm shocked at you! That land has been in his family for years. That land is part of who they are. Steve's grandparents were some of the original settlers in White Lake. That land is their monument and memorial."

"He'll get a fair price," Edward replied, unmoved. Women could get so emotional.

"That family needs more than 'fair'," Corinne objected. "They need help. It feels so… so… well, so greedy to take advantage of someone's misfortune like that. It's like stealing their land out from underneath them. You know that."

Ed leaned forward, animated at the thin accusation. "He *wants* to sell. There's not much he can do with it. The market price is better now than it will be in six months. This way he'll get something to help his family and it frees up the land for someone who can improve its value."

"Meaning Richard 'The Raider' Riceland," Corinne said sarcastically.

"No, meaning Tom Perkins. And me. And you. People who care about this town. We can make big things happen here. Richard Riceland is just a resource to make it happen sooner and better."

"What's wrong with waiting? Going slow usually means fewer mistakes."

"Going slow usually means finishing last and that means fewer rewards," Ed retorted. "This is a different day and age, Corinne. Things move faster in the world and if you want to get all that life has to offer you have to keep up. It's time for White Lake to take that next step forward and move into the 20th century. Even the Bible says, 'The race is to the swift'."

Corinne didn't know for sure, but she doubted the Bible really said that. Ed was no scriptorian and she sensed that when he started quoting scripture, he was running out of ideas. Yet it did sound vaguely familiar. "Where does the Bible say that?"

"It's in there somewhere. I don't know. You don't believe me? You can look it up if you want to, but you know that it is true."

Corinne's mind was racing now and she shifted gears. "And what do you have to promise Riceland? I'm sure he's not interested in this thing just because he thinks motor inn cabins in a remote western town are cute. And I *know* he's not in it out of the goodness of his heart."

"Don't worry about it."

Wrong answer. "That makes me worry about it all the more! How will Riceland extract his pound of flesh from you and Tom Perkins and heaven knows who else if things go sour?"

"They're not going to. Even in our worst-case projections, we come out on top. What's wrong with you? Why are you acting like this?"

"Why are *you* acting like this? All mysterious and unwilling to discuss something that could ruin us forever."

"Oh, stop being melodramatic."

"It's true. Getting mixed up with a Richard Riceland doesn't come without dangers. You're risking our livelihood and you're calling me melodramatic? You could easily get us in over our heads so deep we'd never get out."

"Not one chance in a million."

"And what about the rest of the town? What will they have to pay for Riceland to come in here?"

"Nothing."

"Nothing is for nothing. What about Willie Martin and Ben Thompson? Did they change their minds about this 'race of the swift' to progress?"

Ed was red in the face with frustration. "How many times do we have to go over this? I've been telling you for weeks it doesn't matter what Ben Thompson and Willie Martin say, do or think! What is it about what I've explained that you can't grasp? We don't need them anymore. The project is going to happen whether they like it or not!"

The truth was Corinne hit a raw nerve with her last question. Thompson and Martin had been determined voices of opposition from the start. Since Tom Perkins' courting of Riceland involvement in the project, they had moved from steady persistence to quiet persuasion. Ed knew for a fact that Ben Thompson personally visited other business owners in White Lake and talked some of them out of their endorsement for the Perkins-Whitmore Project, as it had come to be known.

As expected, R. Porter Hatch, bank president turned against it because he was no longer being asked to finance it. Larry Nelson, owner of Sole-Mate Shoe Repair, and Donald Oslow of Oslow Pharmacy already switched. So did Jenny Campbell, owner of Sally's Shop. She was the wife of Jasper Campbell, respected city councilman. The full city council, of course, still had to give final approval to the land use. There was rumor of others trying to get them to delay action. Too much of a delay would mean construction would have to wait until after the harsh winter months and the spring thaw. The extra costs of waiting could kill the whole thing.

The upshot was that whereas a month ago, their approval was considered a foregone conclusion, Ed wasn't so sure now. He was nervous about it. He was glad the Riceland boys were coming in on Thursday. He hoped they had not heard the latest about the erosion of support from the business community in White Lake.

Corinne pushed the issue impatiently. "Well, have they changed their minds or not?"

"No."

"Seems like if these motor inn cabins were such a great deal for White Lake, successful businessmen like Ben Thompson and Willie Martin would be behind it by now."

"Corinne, you are the most annoying person I know! Pester me no longer about matters best left to me! You don't understand all the complicated aspects. I've been working for months on this and now, just as we're set to make the most visionary move in the history of this town, my own soft-headed wife doesn't even support me!"

"Who are you calling 'soft-headed'?" Corinne angrily flamed. "Ed Whitmore, you're so pumped up with your own self-importance … As if building a place for tourists is 'the most visionary move in the history of White Lake.' I'm sure the pioneer founders of the town might have something to say to you about that one!"

"You know what I mean."

"I do know, and I think you're puffing all this up because you're scared."

"Scared?" Ed scoffed. "What have I got to be scared of?"

"Do you think I don't hear the talk going around town? I hear there are a lot of folks against your motor inn cabins now. I think you're scared you won't have enough support to pull it off."

Ed festered in silence.

"Know what else I think?"

"What?" Ed flashed angrily.

"I think you're a coward for not standing up to do right by the Nates, for not standing up to Tom Perkins and his infatuation with Richard Riceland and for not standing up for your family."

Ed rose abruptly from his chair, bumping the table and rattling the dishes in the process. Nobody—especially not his wife—called him a coward. "What do you know about courage?" he shot back loudly. "You're so short-sighted you can't see the obvious at the end of your nose. I can't help it if others around town have the same problem. I'm standing for the future of White Lake. I'm standing for prosperity and growth for everyone, even those who are against us." His voice grew louder and higher pitched as his agitation grew. "They have such small minds, and now I can't believe you are joining them! It's the future I'm interested in. Yours and mine—ours. Why can't you see that? Why do you call that 'cowardice?' You need to support me, like a wife should!"

"What future?" Corinne shot back. "You aren't bringing enough home now for us to live on. There's not going to …"

"I do so," Ed interrupted. "That's not fair. I provide the necessities and some of the comforts of life for you, and always have since we've been married. Just because things are a little tight right now while we get big things going, you start whining about a few little sacrifices we need to make for a month or two. Don't …"

Now Corinne interrupted. "Whining? I don't think it's whining to find out what my husband is doing with our lives. And I don't call having no money to buy the food or pay the bills 'sacrifice.' Something has to change and fast or the plain fact is we're not going to make it!"

"Stop interrupting!" Ed angrily retorted. "As I was saying …"

"You're the one who interrupted me!" Corinne cried. Exasperated, she crossed her arms and asserted, "I'm not going to be treated this way!"

"What way? You started all this aggravation!"

"I was just trying to have a breakfast conversation! Can I help it you get all tense and angry over simple communication? Stop shouting at me!"

"You're the one shouting at me!" Ed exploded. He reached boiling point. "This is ridiculous. I can't be married to a woman who is going to act like this. I'm a businessman and risks are a part of any successful business venture. You knew what I was when you married me!"

"I didn't know you would treat me like this." Corinne started to cry.

Ed hated that because he didn't know how to respond. Deep down he wanted her to feel good about things. Deep down he sensed that she was hurt. But it was her own doing, he angrily reasoned. She should be supportive, not part of the opposition.

"Just go on," Corinne sniffled. "Go do your stupid business, not caring whether it's right or who you hurt." With that last little spiteful remark, she pushed her chair away and turned her back to Ed, wiping wet eyes with her linen napkin.

In some attempt to repair the situation, he walked around the table and touched her tentatively on the shoulder. She desperately wanted to respond warmly, but her anger and hurt loomed too large. Or maybe it was her pride. She wrenched away from him. "Just leave me alone."

He obliged, slamming the door for emphasis on the way out.

Later, Corinne pulled out their family Bible. It took some doing, but she found it. Right there in the Book of Ecclesiastes. 9th chapter, verse 11: "…*the race is _not_ to the swift*…"

ॐ

Corinne was sullen and quiet as she did Sarah Williams' toenails later that afternoon.

Sarah recognized the outward signals of inward struggle and respected her young friend's need to wrestle alone for a while with her thoughts. She knew they must seem very large and frightening because when Corinne massaged her feet she uncharacteristically rubbed them very rapidly and with more intense pressure than her usual gentle touch. In fact, the massage hurt. Sarah winced and looked at Corinne. She saw a young woman, advancing in her first pregnancy, obviously absorbed in her own pain. The old woman endured the rub down, kindly saying nothing.

Corinne finally finished her routine and slipped Sarah's slippers onto the small, withered feet. She carried herself heavily to the sofa across from her old friend and plopped down hard. She sat up erect, fidgeting fingers clasped over her protruding abdomen.

"Honey, I'm going to nominate you to the Nail Nippers Hall of Fame," Sarah smiled weakly. "I do believe you just set a new world's record for the fastest soak, trim and massage in foot care history."

Corinne looked back at the frail, fragile woman and realized what she had done. "Oh, I'm so sorry!" she apologized, genuinely horrified. Recognizing how rough she had been while in her state of self-absorption, she added, "I hope I didn't hurt you."

"Oh, no, dear, you didn't hurt me," Sarah said, "just my feet. But they are like dry little twigs anyway. Almost useless."

Sarah knocked at them with her cane in mock disgust. "They used to be fine, stalwart friends. Now take a look at them. Still, they've done the best they can for an awful lot of years. Like their owner, I'm afraid they're just getting old."

Corinne started to protest, but could not in the face of the obvious. Sarah was noticeably weaker today. She moved more slowly and with greater effort. She experienced more pain. She tired with the least exertion. She did not eat much anymore and so her body dwindled to a stooping shadow of what she was even just a few months ago. The wrinkles of old age hung like dusty drapes from her arms and cheeks and eyes. The decline was alarming to Corinne. Is this what happened when you die of old age? She secretly hoped that when it was her time to go, she could go quickly.

"I am terribly sorry," Corinne again said. "I am too caught up in myself today, I'm afraid."

"What's the matter dear?"

"Oh, nothing really." Corinne was loath to burden the old woman with one particle of her own puny troubles, but instinctively sensed that Sarah needed to be needed. "I'm just so … so … well, I think something must be wrong with me. I'm too selfish, I guess." Corinne rehearsed the morning's squabble with Ed, concluding with, "I just don't feel happy. I feel guilty about that. I know Ed tries. I mean, no one can be happy *all* the time, can they?" she queried hopefully.

Sarah took her time to answer. When she finally spoke, she proceeded deliberately with as strong a voice as she could muster. Looking directly into the bright eyes of the young mother-to-be she said, "Hmmm. Yes. No one can be happy all the time. I heard that old saw when I was young, too. I even pulled it out and consoled myself with it on occasion when life got a little rough and I started feeling sorry for myself."

Corinne nodded, a look of resignation across her face.

"The problem is that it's not true."

"What do you mean it's not true? Were you always happy?"

"Of course I was, and so are you, dear."

Corinne was puzzled. "No, I am not. I …"

"There's nothing wrong with you, dear. When I was young I sometimes confused happiness with other things. I thought comfort was happiness; it's not. I thought security was happiness; it's not. I thought a painless, smooth ride through life was what happiness was supposed to be; it's not. I thought a 'perfect' relationship with James was happiness; it's not. Neither was having the most brilliant children in White Lake. All those things are good and wonderful, but happiness is something within you that transcends them all."

Sarah shifted in her chair, relieving a creeping ache. "Most marriages will never be fairy tales of never ending bliss. They turn out to be rather normal where both people have to work hard and make sacrifices of their own desires and feelings."

Corinne's eyes grew wider with surprise.

"Most kids grow up to be quite ordinary people. Most of the money and land and wealth people accumulate will be small and insignificant and fleeting. The savings of a lifetime can melt away, just evaporate in a moment. Happiness is not any of these things."

"It's not?" Corinne said.

"No, no. You see, my dear, I learned somewhere along the way that life mostly is a bumpy ride on a rocky road. Everyone's journey gets hard. No one is immune to trial and disappointment. But on your ride every once in a while, you get to thrill to a breathtaking scenic view. You reach the top of a mountain or two. You ride along, working hard at it, often hurting and bone-tired, all the while collecting a suitcase load of memories about the trip. The trick is to find joy in the expedition. If you miss the joy, you miss it all."

"That just sounds like dressing up misery in fine clothes and calling it 'joy,'" Corinne responded, petulantly crossing her arms. "I'm not happy all the time and I don't think anyone is."

"Well now, if by happy you mean a life of ease with no problems, then naturally you won't be happy much of the time. If you must constantly keep checking your pulse to see whether or not you're 'happy,' you won't be."

Corinne sat back in the chair and let out a gasp of air.

"Are you all right dear?"

"Yes. I think so. Just feels like a bit of indigestion or something."

"Pregnancy heartburn," Sarah said knowingly.

"Pregnancy heartburn?"

"Yes. Happened to me all the time with my children. What you do is just take a spoonful of bicarbonate soda in a glass of warmish water. That will take care of it."

"Thanks. I'll try it."

"Let me know if it works for you."

Corinne nodded and then continued the conversation. "It's not that I expect everything to be easy…"

"Of course you don't, dear."

"But does it have to be so hard?" Corinne felt childish the second the words rolled impulsively off her tongue.

Sarah chuckled. "Well, dear, if it wasn't who could find the joy? Who would appreciate it? Suppose every sickness were immediately healed, every disaster eliminated and every tragedy averted. Would people really be better off for it? If there was no rain, would we still enjoy the sunshine?"

"I don't know," said Corinne crabbily. She slouched back into the plush sofa, a frown on her face.

Sarah paused thoughtfully. "Do you remember the flood three years ago?"

"Remember it? It was the biggest thing to happen around here during my life. Lots of folks put out of their homes."

"Sounds like a terrible thing. How could those families keep going? How could White Lake survive?"

"Well, people pitched in and helped each other, of course," Corinne said, sitting up again. "We took in the Frazier children while men from the town cleaned up and rebuilt their place out at the mouth of the canyon. Tommy and Janie. I was their babysitter during the day. Little rascals, both of them," Corinne smiled. "They always visit around Christmas time, caroling and a plate of goodies, and that sort of thing."

"Interesting, isn't it? Until something like that happens, folks just sort of stay wrapped up in themselves, coasting along. Adversity opens the windows of the heart to larger possibilities. I dare say the Fraziers would have never become a part of your life until the flood."

"No, you're right, I'm sure," Corinne admitted.

"I've been around a lot of years now," Sarah continued. "A lot of water has passed under this old rickety bridge and I've learned a thing or two about happiness and joy and such. I believe that if everything in your marriage or pregnancy or life went along smoothly without any surprises or bumps according to some perfect fairy tale you've concocted in your mind, you'd be cheated from life's true joys. Like those moments when you feel so close to your husband that you're each one part of the same being. Or when your baby kicks with wondrous energy inside of you. Or when you receive a little appreciation for helping an old woman cut her toenails." Sarah winked and Corinne blushed.

The old woman went on. "Joy is the result of your effort and struggle and faith to overcome. Do you really want to give up these special moments in exchange for complete ease and comfort? Do you really want immunity?"

The idea distilled on Corinne's heart like fresh dew on summer grass. "I guess," she began thoughtfully, "that it's all in the way you choose to see things, isn't it? Finding the joy, I mean."

Sarah smiled. "That's a good point, dear."

"Because I've been looking at things quite selfishly. I want things to be the way I want them, so I try to make things 'right.' Especially with Ed." Corinne gasped with the revelation. "Oh, how can he put up with it? I guess I've missed the bigger picture. The trouble with my making things 'right' all the time, is that sometimes I'm wrong. I don't know everything."

"None of us do. None of us will."

"And another thing," Corinne said earnestly. It was all clicking in her mind now. "While I'm busy making things right, all I'm really doing is trying to protect myself from bad things going wrong. It's like a bird trying to keep her eggs from hatching because she thinks the goal is to have unbroken shells. That's what I'm like! To use your analogy, I think I miss the joy of sunshine because I'm too involved in planning against the rain."

"Interesting, isn't it, how we do that? A little more appreciation and gratitude for simple blessings and pleasures. That's what the world needs."

Corinne's heart raced excitedly with new vision. "By just seeing things a little differently, I guess … Yes! I think I see what you mean. You *can* be happy 'all the time' because you take a longer, more mature view of things. I'm understanding now! So, you end up seeing the small, overlooked blessings for what they are. Kind of small miracles that are wonderful surprises, like warm sunshine breaking through the clouds on a gloomy day."

"Yes. So, you see, if you miss the joy …"

"… you miss it all!"

CB

"Come on, boys! Grab your instruments and let's go! We'll be late for the dance." There was the raucous scrambling of boys' bodies as the Williams clan jumped at their father's command.

"Mom, where's my clarinet?" a frustrated Chris called out.

Sarah was occupied with getting little Maggie's hair combed. James was with the horse and wagon out front, though periodically he poked an impatient head into the house to hurry the stragglers along. She was a little irritated at Chris' question and James' prodding. "I don't know, Chris," she snapped. "Did you look in the living room by the piano?"

"Yes, and it's not there!"

"How about under your bed?"

There was the pounding of rushing feet taking the stairs two at a time as Chris remembered the spot he had failed to search. "Never mind!" he shouted with relief a moment later, "I found it!" The pounding reversed itself as Chris ran back down the stairs.

"Where was it?" Sarah asked, tying the last ribbon in Maggie's hair.

"Under the bed." Chris shot out the front door and hopped into the back of the wagon with his brothers. Frank had Peter in a headlock and wouldn't let go until he squealed like a pig and hollered 'Uncle!' Peter protested to his father, but James ignored the playful roughhousing, anxious for Sarah and Maggie to appear.

"Oh, you look absolutely precious!" Sarah doted. Maggie flashed a pleased grin and pranced merrily ahead of her mother out the door. James modeled the gallantry he wanted his boys to show the fairer sex as he helped both of his girls onto the padded buckboard seats before jumping up himself and grabbing the reins.

"Gee-yup!" The wagon lurched forward, its happy cargo lightheartedly looking forward to the evening's engagement at Center Park.

They were the Williams Family Band. They were going to play the August Summer Social where there would be dancing and ice cream and watermelon. It was a festive, carefree time to which all members of the community came. It had gained in popularity over the years and now included small exhibit booths and games for the little ones. The dance was always the highlight of the evening and for the past two years the Williams Family Band had been the group of choice to play for it. They were the best talent in White Lake and stacked up pretty well against every other dance band in the valley. Jimmy was an especially gifted fiddler and, just months shy of his fourteenth birthday, was already considered a top contender for first prize at the Fiddler's Contest held during the State Fair just two weeks away. Chris was accomplished on the clarinet. Frank handled drums; Peter was learning flute and Merlin the accordion and tenor sax. Maggie was still young, but had obvious natural voice talent and was featured on a number of songs. Sarah was on piano, the thread that held them all together, while James filled in the background with a passable bass. On a few numbers each night, he pulled out his fiddle and he and Jimmy "dueled" on stage. It was a whole lot of fun and the crowds loved it.

They arrived two hours early to set up and to enjoy as a family some of the preliminary activities. Long rows of tables with picnic foods of every variety stood as a tempting invitation to all. The table with cakes and pies was most popular with thick crowds of children of all ages gathered like ants to sugar. The women saved their special treats for last and were secretly pleased when their dishes were the first to be consumed. Large tubs of ice cream, another crowd pleaser, would soon arrive from Poulsen's Dairy.

A baseball game was in progress at the south end of the park. Boys and men magically became the same age as the game progressed and the friendly competition grew keen. Egg tossing and apple bobbing attracted youngsters on the east side of the park.

A few quilts and other homemade crafts were set up for display on the west side, along with a petition for registered voters to sign about restricting the water farmers a hundred miles upstream could take out for irrigation. Folks in the valley had a notion the amount of water coming into White Lake and its streams had been slowly declining because of new farming and this was a way to officially gripe about it.

Parker Thompson organized a group of workers from the store and they were carving thick slices of cool red-meat watermelon under a banner stretched between two young oaks promoting Williams General Mercantile, just south of the pavilion. The watermelon and goodwill were free. Later, James and Sarah came over and personally passed out the delicious treat, a sincere way to say 'thank you' to customers who were friends and to friends who were customers.

Matronly Mrs. Paul danced a little jig upon being handed a bounteous slice by Sarah and exclaimed, "The Summer Social is wonderful! I always look forward for months to it and they get better every year." Looking at James she added, "You know, I feel like a new woman!"

"I do, too, Mrs. Paul," James mischievously responded. "But I'll probably go home with the same old one." He ducked just in the nick of time to avoid Sarah's playful punch.

Meanwhile, the Williams children put their instruments away under the bandstand at the pavilion and went their separate ways to enjoy the activities. They planned to get together again in an hour to set up for the dance. Jimmy and Chris took off to get in an inning or two at the ball game. About fifteen minutes before it was time to meet back with the rest of the family, they heard a big ruckus over at the pavilion and saw a crowd running toward the spot where they were scheduled to perform. They hurried over and checked under the bandstand, relieved to find the instruments undisturbed. They turned their attention to the source of the commotion. A man was shouting, wildly waving a paper in his right hand.

"You cheated me! You're a g__d___'d thief!" Jimmy and Chris slithered through the throng for a better view. It was old Joe Clinton. His three sons stood across the circle from them, arms crossed and sneers on their thin lips. For the moment they were too absorbed with their father's antics to notice Jimmy and Chris. Clinton rattled his paper again and yelled, "I tell all of you, watch out! James Williams is a thief! He stole my land and the water rights with it. No tellin' what he's doin' to you every time you go into his store. He's robbin' us blind, I tell you!"

James Williams felt a hot river of anger surge through his breast. It took every ounce of manly dignity and control not to simply haul off and pop this scruffy loudmouth in the chops to shut him up.

Instead, he turned away from his antagonist and cheerfully addressed the gathered crowd. "Come on, folks. We're all here to have a good time. I'm sure there's a better time and place to take care of whatever Mr. Clinton's issue is. Now the dance is going to start in just a little while here. We'll make some music and have some fun, shall we?"

"Don't you turn your back on me, James Williams!" Clinton's voice rasped with icy rage. " 'Cause if you do, it'll be the last time, that's for sure."

But James continued to ignore his foe, trying to carefully make his way through the mass of people to the bandstand.

"You're just plain yellow!" the man screamed. "You're yellow now just like when you took my land from me." Joe Clinton was not going to let it drop. "Folks, like a yellow-bellied coward he snuck in behind me and stole that land where his store sits today. That piece was supposed to be mine. I've got the signed agreement from old man Jackson before he died to prove it!" He waved the paper he clutched like a victory banner high over his head. "I had the lawful right to buy that property with the rights. It was mine. Mine."

The crowd silently shifted its attention to James. There was no alternative—he would have to give a response. He turned and stared coolly at his adversary. His firm jaw was taut and the look he gave Joe Clinton carried such raw power that the men closest in the circle reflexively stepped back in awe. His voice was strong yet quiet as he spoke. "You know full well, sir, that I bought that land from Mr. Jackson, paid full in cash, in a fair deal. It was offered to me after a certain 'unnamed buyer' reneged on his promise to come up with sufficient funds to secure it. I have the legally registered deed in a safe place. I will meet you Monday morning at the courthouse where we can both review it. We will settle it then. Now let's get the dance started."

There was a murmur of approval from the crowd. He motioned to Jimmy and Chris. "Boys, go get the instruments and set up, will you?"

Joe Clinton, pushed now by anger coupled with a growing sense of humiliation, bawled out, "I say we settle it now!" He took a step toward James, whose back was turned. "First, I'm goin' to beat the livin' tar out of you and then you're gonna give my land back to me!"

James turned and just wearily shook his head.

"See that! Didn't I tell ya' he was a yellow-bellied coward? Come on, Williams. You're just afraid I'll whup you good. Do ya' hear me, you yellow thief?" Clinton's shabby stubble caught the white froth that oozed from the sides of his mouth. He was restrained by a couple of the men as he punched wildly toward James. "I'll tell you what. If you're not too big a coward, I say let's settle this and I'll make it interesting for ya'. We'll do this like the old days. Just you and me, man on man, fightin' it out. You win, and me and my boys leave town and you keep my land. I whip you, and you just hand me back what's mine anyhow. What do ya' say, James Williams. You too yellow, or have we got a deal?'

"No deal, Joe. Only a fool plays another man's game. I'm no fool."

"We'll see about that!" He struggled to break the grasp of the men holding him back, yelling curses and threats at James. James calmly stood his ground.

"Hey, now, what's going on here?" Niles Jensen, the sheriff, finally muscled his way through the mob and confronted the two rivals. "Come on, boys. Break it up. This isn't the time or place."

Joe quit straining and glowered at James. "Nuthin's happenin' here, Sheriff. Ain't that right, Williams?"

James looked at Sheriff Jensen with the idea of explaining it all, but thought better of it. "Joe here was just presenting me with a little surprise before we go on stage tonight."

"All right, boys. I see that neither one of you is going to tell me about it, so what do you say we just call it even and go on with the social? James, come on, you've got a dance to play. Joe, you and your boys move along now. Come on, folks, it's all over here. Go on and get some ice cream. The dance will be ready to start in just a little while." Niles pushed the crowd along, breaking them up. "That's it. That's right. Everybody just move on and enjoy yourselves now."

Jimmy and Chris headed to the back of the pavilion and began removing the family's instruments from the crawl space under the bandstand. The twins spoke little but knew each other's mind. They were mighty proud of the way their dad acted when provoked by Joe Clinton. They had no doubt that, if forced to, he would have taken the mean old goat on. Would have whipped him, too. But their father was a bigger man than that and they figured he had proved it in spades to everybody in town who didn't know it before. The boys unabashedly esteemed him as a real hero.

The snarling just outside the crawl space door suddenly interrupted the twins' work. "You know, you slimy little critters, this ain't over." It was Zeb, the oldest of the three Clinton boys. His brothers stood behind him, their arms still crossed and those perpetual sneers still pasted on their lips.

Jimmy and Chris glanced at each other. Their predicament was clear. With the only way in and out of the space blocked, they were trapped. They each knew what they had to do. Clutching fast to Peter's flute case, Jimmy crawled out first, followed closely by Chris on his hands and knees. Before they could stand erect the Clinton boys surrounded them.

"Maggots turn into flies," Zeb growled, "an' a Williams boy'll become a no account thief like his pa." Jimmy and Chris rose slowly to their feet and stood back to back. For the first time they could see the wooden rod, a full two inches in diameter, that the elder Clinton boy held threateningly in his hand. "We aim to give you the beatin' your pa woulda had from our pa if'n the sheriff hadn't come along." He motioned with a nod to his brothers. "Boys, let's give it to 'em!"

The Clinton boys grinned with evil delight and closed in on their prey. There wasn't time for the twins to do anything but react. As Zeb raised his stick above his head, Jimmy quickly lunged at his foe, ramming the hard case holding Peter's flute into the older boy's gut. Zeb doubled over, moaning loudly and gasping for breath. Fast as lightening Jimmy zipped past Zeb with Chris right behind.

The younger Clinton brothers, Abe and Hack, were caught off guard by the twin's speed and lurched awkwardly forward to catch their intended quarry, but ran into their big brother. Chris, keeping his wits about him, planted his foot firmly on Zeb's backside and shoved for all he was worth. Zeb lunged forward, landing on top of his bewildered brothers, sending all three sprawling. It gave Jimmy and Chris the break they needed to sprint around to the other side of the pavilion and hop up onto the bandstand where, in full view of the milling crowd, they would be safe. After the public spectacle their fathers just made, not even the Clinton boys would be stupid enough to come on stage to start something now.

Hands on knees, the twins took a moment to catch their breath. The terror of danger brings out a gamut of emotions and the twins burst out laughing in the relief of escape. "Did you hear that old bear bellow when you caught him that good one in the breadbasket?" Chris guffawed.

"And did you hear him howling when you kicked his fanny?" Jimmy chortled.

"And how about Zeb rolling into his brothers ..."

"... like a bowling ball into pins!" they finished together.

James and Sarah brought the rest of the Williams children on stage to finish the setup. "What's so funny, boys?" their father asked.

"Oh, nothing, I suppose," Jimmy responded grinning broadly.

"Come on, come on. You tell me nothing is funny when you two are up here all giddy like a couple of giggling girls?"

The twins laughed all the harder at the image evoked by the comparison.

There was a lot to do to get ready for the dance and Sarah was in no mood to put up with such light-mindedness. "Let's go, boys. Stop playing around. Jimmy, get your fiddle and get tuned up. And put enough resin on your bow. We're playing long sets tonight. Chris, get your guitar ready. We're starting with square dancing first. Come on now, hop to it!"

Chris winked at Jimmy and they hurried off to obey their mother. There was no arguing with her when she got into her "business" mood.

"I believe those Clinton boys just invented a dance of their own," Jimmy sniggered quietly to his brother.

"Yep, the 'Fall Down Polka'," Chris quipped gleefully back.

"I heard that," James interrupted. "What've you two been up to? Did you have a run in with Joe Clinton's boys?"

"I wouldn't call it a run in exactly," Jimmy meekly replied.

"More like a run away," Chris tried to explain.

"How many times have I told you those Clinton boys are up to no good," James continued firmly. "Now tell me what happened."

Jimmy and Chris related the story. James held in the laughter at the description of their daring escape, trying in vain to keep a properly stern face.

Sarah was far from amused. "We've told you before to stay away from those boys," she scolded. "I have a very bad feeling about them. They're big trouble."

"We *did* stay away," Chris said.

"They came looking for us. Trapped us in the crawl space under the pavilion when we were getting the instruments," Jimmy added. "We didn't do anything wrong."

"Your mother's right," James cut in, "and I don't want to hear anymore of your talking back to her."

"No, sir," they said in unison.

James leaned down, put one hand on each of his boys' shoulders and winked. In a low voice only they could hear he added, "But those bullies had it coming to them!"

"James!" Sarah barked. She flashed him The Look and he quickly straightened up.

"Okay. Snap to it! Let's get the show on the road!' James commanded.

Soon they were tuned up and ready to go. After a brief introduction by Samuel H. Perkins, White Lake's esteemed mayor, James looked at Jimmy and said, "Here we go, boy. Fiddle for all it's worth! One, two, three, four!"

The Williams Family Band launched energetically into their opening number entitled "Devil's Dream," a fast-moving, old-time, toe-tapping tune that always got the crowd clapping and swinging and laughing. They played all night and the people danced.

The report in the next local weekly made no mention of the Joe Clinton-James Williams debacle at the summer social. Instead, it rehearsed the events of the day, gave the baseball score, and praised the band. It summed up the joyous occasion this way: *A good time was had by all.*

⌘

Friday, August 2.

I visited Sarah Williams today and did her toenails. I'm worried about her. She has periods when she doesn't know who I am or thinks I'm her daughter Maggie. Sarah says Maggie is coming to visit. I don't know if that's true or not. She is weaker and can't get around like she used to and I'm afraid she is not eating much at all. I told her I would come by every day to check on her. Some days she seems fine and others are worse. She still tells me stories about her and James and the twins and the others. I love that. She's always good for a story. I learn so much from them, and I really think it helps me get through this pregnancy.

I'm getting pretty fat now. I can't describe how it feels to know a little person is growing inside of me. It is an amazing, remarkable thing, a genuine miracle of sorts. Imagine me, part of a miracle. Who would have thought? But I _am_ getting fat. Edward doesn't think so. He says I look more beautiful than ever. I don't know how he can think that, but I'm glad he tells me anyway. He really can be sweet when he wants to be.

Edward is struggling terribly with the Riceland deal. I know he is having second thoughts and I'm afraid it's because of me. I've been a little negative about it. I should probably just let him take care of it on his own and have faith he will make the right decision, but I have a bad feeling about it that just won't go away. By the way, I checked on his Bible quote that "the race is to the swift." I found it in Ecclesiastes 9:11. It says, "The race is _not_ to the swift." Even though I'm right, it doesn't seem important now. I'm sure he'll do the right thing.

All in all, I realize life is good. As Sarah says, "If you miss the joy, you miss it all." The fifth secret.

Chapter Seven

Our lives are not our own.

"Sometimes I just can't comprehend you," Corinne blurted in exasperation.

"That's all right," Ed replied, a wry smile barely escaping the corners of his mouth. "If you'd wanted someone more comprehensible, you'd have married yourself."

Corinne popped with laughter.

"Hey, at least I'm cute." Ed held out his arms.

Like a magnet, Corinne leaned toward him. "Now how can a girl resist 'cute' compared to 'comprehensible'?" She wrapped her arm into his and clasped her delicate hand in his large, strong one. "I love you, Ed Whitmore."

"I love you, too, dear."

"So what are you going to do?" Corinne's voice edged with concern.

"I'm not sure just yet."

She took one step away so she could better look at his face. "You see, that's what I don't understand. You've put so much work into the motor inn project and the Riceland deal. Now, to even think about pulling out …"

"You're a funny girl," Ed chuckled. "I thought you didn't want me to go ahead. I seem to remember you were the one who called Richard Riceland 'The Raider'? And what about those bad feelings you had about the project?"

"Not about the project, just about the deal. A bad feeling about the deal. And it was the paper who nicknamed him, not me."

"Okay. A bad feeling about the deal. Of course, there is no project without the deal."

"Still, you've put so much into it and you're getting so close to the end. Seems a shame to change your mind now."

"I haven't said anything about changing my mind. I'm just evaluating the options, that's all."

"Why now?"

"Well, actually, I've been thinking all along. Starting when the bank was reluctant to finance the deal. And Ben Thompson and Willie Martin. And the fact that time's starting to slip away, and with commissions dropping and all …" Edward hesitated and shook his head wistfully. It was the start of autumn—almost too late to begin construction and still no sight of Richard Riceland's money. He wanted to get all the fine print sorted out, according to his boys. Edward's natural skepticism made him wonder. Then he snapped his head up, looked Corinne in the eye and playfully wagged, "Your 'advice' has not fallen on deaf ears, you know." Then more seriously he queried, "Have your feelings changed?"

"Changed?" Corinne paused. It dawned on her that something *had* changed. But what? Not her uneasiness about Richard Riceland. That had always lingered like raw onions on the breath. No matter how much she tried to sweeten it up with Ed's enthusiastic promise of a brighter future, she could not get rid of the nagging taste that something was not quite right about it.

Maybe what had changed was her feeling about Edward. Her fresh idealism as a young, new bride had wilted a bit the past few months under the heat of day-to-day life's struggle. Making a living wasn't as easy for her husband as she at first naively supposed. Making a life demanded even more. As the project bogged down and his commissions dwindled to a trickle, they experienced great financial pressure. Edward's fears and self-doubts surfaced. That had surprised her. He had seemed so much like her knight in shining armor before they were married. She imagined then he was just about perfect. 'Happily ever after,' she was certain, would not be a fairy tale with them.

Yet now she saw that her knight had doubts stalking his determination like dark shadows. Could it be, she wondered, that his armor was nothing more than the brave smile and persistent attitude he made himself put on every day? He was not, she realized, a mythical prince who slew all her ugly dragons and made her life magical and easy and totally comfortable. Edward, it turned out, was simply a man like other men. Like other men he dreamed large dreams, while yet tethered to the dreary yoke of daily duty. Her proximity to his merely mortal capacity, however, had served to deepen her love for him, not diminish it. She was proud of him, even if he could not be of himself. Her feelings of admiration and respect and true love had surely intensified, but, she concluded, had not really changed.

So had anything changed? Then it struck her. What had changed were not her feelings about Richard Riceland or the project or her husband. Rather, it was she who had changed. It wasn't just the fact that she was pregnant, though that was a big part of it. It was... well, she had matured. That was it. She no longer viewed herself through the superficial spectacles of childhood. Somewhere along the way—she wasn't sure just when—she had shed them in favor of the more powerful lenses of her grown womanhood. She was finally an adult with adult views and adult problems and adult possibilities. It felt odd to her that she wasn't a kid any more. Of course, Sarah Williams had helped her immensely. But when did it happen? The change in her feelings had occurred imperceptibly, unnoticed for the most part until this moment when Edward's question caused her to stop and think.

"Yes," she finally answered. "Yes, I must say my feelings have changed."

Edward arched his right brow in mild surprise. "Really? How?"

"I just realize you are a finer man than I ever understood. I don't think you see how wonderful you are and can be. I love you for how strong and good you are. And I respect you so much more for getting up every day to go fight the battles you face in doing right by us."

Edward was obviously humbled yet pleased by his wife's kind words. He stood up and crossed over to her. "Well, you're worth it. And so is our baby." He gave her a warm squeeze. "And whatever happens with the cabins or the deal, I'll do my best to make you proud."

Corinne wrapped an arm around his firm waist and drew him as close to her as her growing abdomen allowed. He leaned down and they kissed tenderly and passionately. This is what heaven is, Corinne thought. Heaven is this moment extended forever.

"I love you," he whispered.

Corinne laid her head against his breast. "I love you, too." Then lifting her head and looking into his eyes she added, "All I want is for you to want me, for us to be one, to share together whatever life has in store for us. Like Sarah says, 'Love not shared …'"

" … 'is no love at all'," Edward finished.

Corinne smiled and gave him a big loving squeeze.

They were interrupted by someone knocking. Edward broke away, walked through the kitchen and the living room to the front door. Corinne was still in her sleeping clothes, trapped in the kitchen. She hoped Ed would quickly send their guest on his way.

"Come in! Come in!" Corinne gasped as she heard her husband's cheerful voice. She shrank nervously into the farthest corner. The thought of company seeing her in the morning, in her nightgown, and with her hair undone absolutely horrified her. Surely Edward would think of that.

"Honey! Guess who is here? It's Ben Thompson. You know, from Williams' General."

143

"Oh, no," she groaned to herself. Keeping her wits about her, she spied her full-length apron hanging on the pantry door. She pulled it around her neck and tied the strings. Next, she briskly ran her fingers through her soft, brown hair, combing it as best she could. Gathering her courage, she straightened herself and walked into the family room.

"Ben, you know my wife Corinne. Corinne, Ben Thompson."

"Yes, so nice to see you again," Ben smiled as he enthusiastically extended a handshake to his hostess.

"Yes, nice to see you, too, Mr. Thompson."

"Why, thank you. And, please, call me Ben."

"Welcome to our home, Ben."

Edward spoke. "Well, this is an unexpected surprise, Ben. Would you like to sit down?"

Ben sat in the overstuffed armchair, which was Ed's favorite. "Thank you," he replied. "This is a nice home you have here, Mrs. Whitmore."

"That's kind of you to say."

"I'm sure you're wondering why I'm here."

"Well, Ben, I don't think you've come asking to buy more insurance. So I'm supposing it has to do with the motor inn cabins project." Ed crossed his arms and leaned back.

"Uh huh. Let me come straight to the point. Ed, I've been watching you as you've worked on this motor inn project. Now you know I'm not in favor of it and that's just the way it is for now."

Ed opened his mouth to protest defensively, but Ben's upraised hand stopped him. "Now, now, I didn't come to your home to engage in a debate about the project. But like I said, you're a smart man, energetic, young, visionary. You're someone who is obviously going places. I've come to offer you a business proposal."

Ed sat a little more erect, his curiosity aroused. Ben Thompson was one of the most respected business leaders in the entire valley. His keen eye and shrewd sense of the valley's market had enabled him to rise quickly in the Williams organization until now he had charge of the entire enterprise, which was vast by regional standards. "I'm listening. What did you have in mind?"

"I spoke with Sarah Williams and she agrees. We could use a man of your caliber. As you may know, Williams General is expanding very rapidly. We have plans not only for White Lake and the valley, but also for the whole state and then throughout the region. It's an undertaking that is too large for one man to manage alone. I need an intelligent businessman to work with me, to learn the ropes and take over day-to-day operations. Ed, you're the one I want. You are that man."

Ed sat back astonished. He glanced over at his wife and the look in Corinne's eyes registered the same surprise. "Let me get this straight. You're offering me a job?"

"Not a job. An opportunity. A place to apply your considerable talent to make an impact in White Lake, to contribute to the growth of the valley and beyond. We want an executive who wants to make big things happen in a positive way."

Ed nodded his head. It was a fact Ben Thompson was visionary, an entrepreneur whose large dreams looked beyond small time profits to building a retail empire. A lot of folks would prosper along with him. It was flattering that a man of Ben's stature and integrity would try to recruit him.

Yet he also knew Ben Thompson was clever and, for whatever reason, was opposed to the motor inn cabins. Perhaps the offer was merely an adroit tactic to derail it.

"What about the cabins?"

"Ed, Corinne," Ben began carefully, "I know you have invested much of yourselves into your project—your time, talent, energy, perhaps money. You and Tom Perkins have put together an impressive, forward-looking concept. As I said before, it is your work on the project that caught my eye and started me thinking about you for an executive slot with our company."

Ed's intensity ratcheted up a notch and he leaned forward. "Then why have you been against the idea from the start? We'd be in construction today if it weren't for you!"

Ben smiled calmly. The young man's passion pleased him greatly. "What you don't realize is that I've never been against the idea."

Ed let out an exasperated gasp. "What? Come on, Ben, everyone knows that you and Willie Martin were the only ones in the beginning who …"

Ben raised a gentle hand of interruption. "I repeat, I have never been against the *idea* of the cabins. Talk to your boss. He'll tell you. Not only am I not against bringing motor inn cabins to White Lake, I think they ought to be built in strategic places throughout the valley as well. For that matter, expand the concept statewide. It would bring outside dollars into our economy, to be sure."

"Then why …"

Ben didn't hear the young man and continued. "I visited months ago with Tom Perkins about it. I even told him I might be interested personally in investing in something like that. He was too focused on getting this piece going over on the Nate property. Didn't connect with the bigger possibilities." Ben looked straight into his young friend's eye. "But you do, don't you Ed?"

It was true. He did see. Yet he was confused by the new information he was hearing from Ben. "I don't understand." He looked searchingly over at Corinne. She mutely shrugged her shoulders. She was thrilled with what she was hearing and could scarcely contain herself, but knew Ed had to sort this news out first on his own. She wisely sensed now was not yet the time for her to speak. She would have plenty to add when it came to actual decision-making time. Turning back to Ben, Ed continued, "Then why…?"

"Why did I speak out against the plan you and Tom have?"

"Yes."

"James and Sarah Williams."

"The Williams? Tell me what you mean."

"While James was alive, he and Sarah helped the family who owns the land you want to get established."

"You mean the Nates," Corinne interjected.

"Yes, the Nate family. Like many folks in these parts, they came here looking for a better way of life. They all were dependent on each other to one degree or another for their survival. The Williams grew their business on the patronage of families just like the Nates. They worked together. They watched out for each other's children, they built this town together. They helped each other through good times and bad. When you have customers like that, you tend to fight for their interests. In turn, they become fiercely loyal to you."

"So what has that got to do with Tom Perkins' and my offer to buy a few acres from Steve Nate along Highway 30? He controls the property now and we named a fair price. We aren't aiming to steal anything," Ed growled.

Corinne wanted to scream at her husband's thick headedness.

Ben replied delicately. "As a businessman, I understand the need to keep costs low. Any good capitalist would attempt to negotiate for the very lowest possible price to protect his interest and that of his investors."

"That's right," Ed agreed. Ben was speaking his language now.

"Yet over the years, James and Sarah Williams learned another business principle. Claimed it was the key to their success. They applied it rigorously, even though on the surface it seems to be something of a paradox. The most important thing is they figured out it works, so they used it."

"Well what is it?" Ed wanted to know.

"Just this: 'Always put service and people first. The money will take care of itself.'"

"That's all?"

"Simple, I know, but how many businessmen do you know who actually apply it?"

Ed had to admit that very few gave more than passing lip service to the notion. Business was for profits. Making money was at the core of their methods. If service had to be shaved a bit to drive lower costs or improve margins, the money came first.

"The customers of Williams General are like family. They come first," Ben continued. "It's honored for generations. So even though Steve Nate is the grandson of the original Nates who started to do business with James and Sarah, the loyalty extends to them, too. To Sarah, he's still family. That land is worth two or three times what you've negotiated."

So that was it. Ben, as an agent for Sarah Williams, opposed the project because the Perkins/Whitmore offer, like any business offer, tried to get as much as it could for as little as it could. Smart business. The mathematics were not lost on Ed, "But if we paid Steve Nate all that Sarah Williams wanted us to, we could never get the financing anywhere to get the project going!"

"Taking advantage of someone else's hard times is no way to build your enterprise," Ben countered. "It's a matter of honor and integrity. Steve Nate and his little family are like family," Ben Thompson repeated.

"And so you're watching out for him." He didn't intend it to, but his tone sounded a bit sarcastic. Corinne pinched the back of his arm, though Ben couldn't see it.

"We watch out for each other," Ben affirmed. He stood abruptly. "Well, time for me to be going. You think about my offer. If you're interested, we can work out an arrangement that would be beneficial to us all. You think it over." He stood and bowed his head slightly at Corinne. "Ma'am, thank you for your hospitality. Ed, take your time. When you're ready, let me know your decision."

Ben Thompson turned and walked briskly out the front door.

 C3

Corinne was as gentle as she could be with Sarah's feet. It was the late fall of the year and for the past few months it was terribly plain to see that her frail, shriveled frame was fading—the source of no little irritation to the strong woman who had accomplished so much. "This old body just hasn't much more to give," she noted.

Corinne did not reply and kept at her task. Her recent deftness with the nail nippers was a far cry from her clumsy attempts that first time on a cold day last February. It all seemed so natural to her now, almost second nature. The routine had expanded over time: first, the warm water soak, then the tender drying with a soft towel; next, the careful trimming of the toenails, after that filing and shaping, followed by a massage and finally the application of soothing, sweet lotion. And, of course, there was the glorious conversation, during which Sarah always supplied some gem of wisdom and insight. Corinne eagerly looked forward to these precious times with Sarah.

The same was true for the old woman. The fact was that with her husband gone and her family moved away, she was lonely. Oh, there was an occasional letter from one of her children or a grandchild. All of them lived so far away, and Sarah almost never saw them, although Maggie had mentioned something about coming out this Christmas.

Of course, Ben Thompson came over to the house about once a week. They talked business. Sarah enjoyed that. He was tremendously capable and could certainly handle Williams Enterprises without her, so she was deeply appreciative of the respect he accorded her by discussing the affairs of the company with her.

She had long been esteemed and sought out by folks in the valley as someone with an extraordinary business sense. Her influence and reputation had grown over the years and was at its peak during the two decades James served as a State Senator. He was immensely popular, too. When he died, more than 3,000 people attended the funeral. For a few months following the service, people visited or called every day, some to talk, some to do business, and others just to 'pay their respects to the Widow Williams." Gradually, they moved on with their own affairs and the visits and contacts ceased.

It was not like it used to be. No one sought her out anymore to ask for her advice. It seemed to her that now, except for Ben Thompson and Corinne Whitmore, she was merely a forgotten relic of the past.

Forgotten and lonely.

That was why she very much looked forward to Corinne's visits, maybe even a little more than she did to Ben Thompson's. Ben was business. Oh, he was personable and all that—that wasn't it. In fact, he was like family to her. But there was no escaping the business element in their relationship and that was okay with both of them.

With Corinne it was different. There was an intimacy, a bond between them that bridged the span of their generations. They were two souls alike who happened to have been born many years apart, best friends even though Corinne was just beginning her adult life and Sarah was just ending hers.

Her feet felt warm and wonderful as Corinne rubbed the sweet-smelling lotion on them. "Strange, isn't it?" she asked her young companion.

"What is, Sarah?" With her task completed, Corinne stood and arched her back. The baby was getting larger and she felt the strain in the lower part of her spine.

"How little we know."

"Hmm. Yes," Corinne nodded, although she didn't *really* know how little she knew. She was sure Sarah would clarify the mystery.

"My life turned out so much differently than I ever would have imagined when I was your age," Sarah continued. "I guess I thought I'd simply be a rancher's wife living my days out in Marshville, raising my children, working the daily chores, going to church on Sunday. I would have been satisfied with a simple life like that. Back then I figured I'd be doing my living and praying and dying pretty much like my parents and their parents before them had done. How little I knew."

"Yet you've accomplished so much. Your life has been amazing!" Corinne gushed.

"Well, thank you, dear. It's tempting to take credit for some of the wonderful things that happened for James and me."

"But you *should* take the credit, Sarah," Corinne persisted. "You worked so hard. You're so talented and smart. You worked to have a wonderful marriage. You worked to rear wonderful children. You had to earn your success in business and the respect you won in the community. You became wealthy because of the actions you and James took. Why wouldn't you take credit for all you've accomplished? You deserve it!"

"Some people would say James and I were just lucky."

"You don't believe that, do you?"

Sarah shifted slightly in her chair as she pondered a response. "No. I don't suppose I do. Luck is a random thing without regard to effort. For James and me, it was all more like farming. You plow, you plant, you nurture and then you harvest. It's that old maxim, 'You reap what you sow'."

"That's what I mean," Corinne picked up, "you did the work. You earned and reaped the rewards. You're a wonderful example to me and others in White Lake. You're amazing! You deserve the credit, Sarah, and whether you want it or not, that's the way I think."

"No, not really, my dear. I don't and neither does James."

"Oh, Sarah!" Corinne gently chided. "What am I going to do with you?"

"Child, listen to me. I understand you, for I used to think the same way. I used to think you could chart your life in a straight line like a paved highway and if you only worked hard enough and kept your eye on your destination, you would eventually arrive."

"I think that's true," Corinne observed.

"Yes, dear. At some level, that is true. Yet there is something more, a law of life higher and larger than setting and achieving your goals."

"What is that?"

"It comes down to learning that our lives are not our own."

"What do you mean, 'our lives are not our own'?" Corinne was genuinely perplexed.

"It's a higher way of living, my dear," Sarah explained. "It's true James and I worked hard. So did everyone else. Of course we did our best to be good parents and good people. All parents do. We tried to guide our lives by giving service to others in everything we did. It was in giving service that we came to know there was a better way."

"A better way?" It suddenly occurred to Corinne that she was starting to sound like a parrot, repeating back everything Sarah said. It momentarily annoyed her to realize that about herself, but her intense curiosity compelled her to say it anyway. And it didn't seem to bother Sarah.

"Let me show you," Sarah continued. "Would you be so kind as to go into the entryway for a moment? Go ahead, dear."

Corinne was puzzled but stood and did as the old woman requested. "All right, Sarah. I'm standing in the entryway. Now what?"

"Do you see the glass case with the musical instruments?"

"Yes. I see them. A violin and a clarinet."

"Yes. Now open the case and bring them to me, if you can, my dear."

Corinne carefully tugged at the glass door on the cabinet. It opened easily without a sound. Gingerly she reached in and retrieved the clarinet. The silver metalwork on the ebony tube was tarnished. The instrument obviously had not been played in years and Corinne wondered if it was worth anything. She carried it to Sarah, placed it in her frail lap, and then returned for the violin.

The violin was a beautiful thing. Corinne peered through an F-hole, tilting it back and forth until the light caught the identifier tag glued to the inside back. It was an old instrument, handmade by an artisan, whose name she couldn't quite make out, in New York more than seventy years ago. "Ed would love this," Corinne thought as she gently wiped away the dust that it had accumulated. Her husband, while not a professional, had learned to play as a boy. Sometimes, especially if he was under a lot of pressure from work, he pulled out his violin and played. It was always to himself, for himself, and if Corinne came into the room while he was playing, he stopped and acted embarrassed. She didn't know why. She thought he was pretty good at it.

Corinne held the violin by the neck and took the bow from the case. She closed the door and brought bow and instrument back to Sarah, who still had the clarinet sitting in her lap. "Okay. Here you go, Sarah. Now what?"

Sarah didn't speak for a long time as she rubbed a bony, frail hand over the curved sides of the violin. She held it up to her cheek and ear, plucking on the strings and adjusting the pegs to tune it. She breathed in deeply, almost a sigh. The polished, rich wood gave an aromatic scent that brought back vivid memories to the old woman. Finally, she quietly said, "Here, my dear. I want you to take these." She held them toward her young friend.

"Okay, Sarah. Would you like me to put them back in the case in the entryway?"

"No, dear. I mean you take them. Keep them. Use them. Do what you want with them. I'm giving them to you."

Corinne was shocked. "But why, Sarah?"

"Because you can do more with them than I can. They belong someplace where they can do some good."

"Well, thank you," Corinne stammered. "Are you sure, Sarah? What about your children? Shouldn't you pass these along to them? I'm sure they have more meaning ..."

"Horse feathers!" Sarah interrupted. "They live too far away. Besides, they have their own instruments and I want to give these to you. I'm certain about this. If you don't take them, I'll be very offended and hurt."

Corinne didn't want to upset her old friend. "Why thank you, Sarah," she said again. "I don't know what to say."

"You've said enough, child," Sarah replied. "The look in your eyes is enough for me and tells me you will use them well."

"What was it you were going to show me? About 'our lives are not our own'?"

"Give your life away, my dear," Sarah counseled. "Give it away in service to others, for that is how James and I learned the higher law I told you about. Of course, dear, it's only when you actually own your life that you can give it away. If it's not yours, you don't have it to give."

"I know that about things like dinner plates and bottled peaches," Corinne responded, "but I never thought about it that way when it comes to my life."

"Well, it's like this, my dear. When you take control of your choices, when you become master of your own life, you 'own' in the way I'm meaning. It is then that you can give it away to someone who can do more with it than you can."

Corinne nodded. "Like the music instruments you gave me. She bit pensively on her lower lip, hesitant to voice the question in her heart. Finally she took courage. "Sarah, to whom did you give your life? Your husband?"

Sarah laughed. "No. James would get a big chuckle hearing that!" Then, more seriously, she added, "No. You're right. No one in the world could do more with my life than me."

Corinne was puzzled again at Sarah's enigmatic point. "So who was it?"

"Someone not in this world, of course—God."

"God?"

"Yes, my dear. When I turned over my music instruments to you, I know you can do so much more with them than I can at this point in my life. When James and I handed our lives to God, we found out that He could make a lot more out of them than we ever could alone. He expanded our horizons. He increased our joys. He added upon our blessings. James and I lived lives that were not our own because we finally understood they belonged to God. We did not seek to become rich, but He allowed that to happen for His reasons. We did not seek for James to become a State Senator, but the service came calling James because our lives were not our own. We did not intend for many of the wonderful things that happened to us to happen to us. God had his purposes and we simply tried to go along with that. Our lives are not our own."

Corinne rubbed her hand across the old violin, much as Sarah had done moments ago before giving it to her. "That's the higher law?"

"Yes. It's all about losing yourself in the service of others. It's all about letting Him use you for His objectives. You do that, my dear, and everything else takes care of itself—your marriage, your children, the places you live, the people you come to know, the money, the work, the service—everything. Our lives are not our own."

❦

The next couple of years were good to the Williams family. They became truly wealthy by valley standards. James and Sarah determined to acquire land at every chance they could afford, along with the water rights that went with it. They picked up some bargains here and there, mostly on properties considered to be without value by most folks, like the rocky, arid mountainous acreage northwest of town. Other land they bought from families moving away from the valley, always paying full price. Often they paid more to help these folks out, most of whom were friends and customers who had hit on hard times and were moving on. The store prospered greatly and they used the growing profits to finance their real estate enterprises, paying cash for every purchase. In time they controlled almost one out of every eight acres in and around White Lake.

The Christmas tradition with Sarah's candy continued until it became legendary. The twins a few years back made it a special project of theirs and had soon recruited other youngsters to help with deliveries. Their next step was to include a few other goods with the candy, like woolen scarves for the new family up on Dornbush Creek, and beef jerky for the Carters. Gradually others who were doing well in White Lake made some donations to the twins and the project took on a life of its own bringing holiday cheer to giver and receiver alike. Yet no matter how many other items were included, the main delight was always Sarah's famous candy.

The family was growing up. All of the children were doing well, excelling in school and other activities. They all had friends, and all were very happy, except every once in a while when Maggie complained Merlin teased her about the lice in her hair. There were never really any lice, but Merlin got a lot of pleasure getting his little sister all riled up over it.

James had been persuaded by some of his best customers to run for the State senate seat formerly held by Tom Clemens. Senator Clemens had retired to his farm between Marshville and White Lake. The only declared candidate was Gregory Pittman, who was from the far north end of the valley up past Mountain View. His idea was to legalize gambling in the area and liquor by the drink. That played well among the rougher element that formed the Mountain View community, but horrified the people in the lower valley.

Pittman also wanted to divert the upstream creeks for mining operations. That could leave ranchers and farmers in the valley without sufficient water to irrigate for livestock and crops. Businesses that supplied the agricultural sector with goods, including Williams General, could be hurt. Pittman's proposal could decimate the livelihood of the lower valley and something had to be done about it. After a town meeting, James Williams emerged as the answer in the minds of most people and so he was asked to oppose Pittman in the election. James was reluctant, but agreed out of a sense of duty.

Not everything came easy and not everyone supported James and Sarah. There were those who believed Joe Clinton's claim to the land Williams General stood on and they held it against James that he had come in behind Joe and bought the land from old man Jackson. Some voted against James in that first election because of it. Others who didn't like the land deal, voted for him anyway, because they couldn't abide the thought of Gregory Pittman representing them at the State capital.

Meanwhile, Joe Clinton moved with his boys to Mountain View, where it was said he was working in a blacksmith shop by day and given to drinking at night. Not surprisingly, he campaigned for Greg Pittman or, rather, against James Williams. He aggressively escalated his tale of having been wronged by James and the Pittman campaign was an easy platform to stump from. The memory of the scene a year ago at the pavilion in Center Park still smarted. He had sworn that night to get revenge. This was one way to get back at the man who he accused of stealing from him.

To begin with, Joe Clinton tried to make his case in court. But Judge Swenson had ruled in James' favor, quickly dismissing Clinton's claim. The fact was, there was no legal basis to the idea that old man Jackson had to sell his land to Clinton even if they had discussed price. Nothing had actually been agreed to, the court found, and so there was no binding covenant between Jackson and Clinton. Therefore the subsequent sale to Williams was perfectly permissible and legal. Joe Clinton was angered by the decision and violently attacked James and the judge in the courtroom. He was restrained, fined and jailed for 30 days. Shortly after his release he moved to Mountain View.

But he had not given up. Tied to a political contest now, Clinton's campaigning had deeply divided the town and region over the matter. Even some of James' friends were persuaded by the stories to see a dark streak to his business practices. It was difficult for James to understand why they would believe the lies told about him and it caused him much sorrow to see them turn against him. He and Sarah often talked late into the night torn up inside about how some people would be so gullible to believe the Pittman-Clinton lies about him. More than once he talked with her about dropping out of the race altogether. Politics, it seemed, was nasty business and took a thick hide. James was too much of a straight shooter and the barbs and innuendos hurt deeply.

Persuaded by his supporters and encouraged by Sarah, James stuck it out. When the final results were tallied it wasn't even close. He won by a landslide. He won every election he ran in after that and some years wasn't even opposed. One year the other side had a candidate, but the opponent decided he was going to vote for James Williams instead of himself. The people appreciated the honesty and integrity of James. He was never in it for himself. He was a man of and for the people he represented and they rewarded him by sending him back to the State capitol year after year.

Through it all, the business prospered and the family band played on. Sarah noticed that James loved the band. More than any other success in his life, his family was his greatest source of delight. The band was a happy way they shared that joy together. They were in great demand and with James' election, their fame grew throughout the state.

Joe Clinton did not give up after the election. His bitterness over the land he thought he was cheated out of festered and his hatred of James Williams grew. His three boys learned from their pa. Whenever they came down from Mountain View into White Lake, they took special delight in going around town until they found the Williams' twins so they could taunt and tease and bully. They were unmerciful. Jimmy and Chris stayed cool and generally let it all roll off their backs, but it was no fun. As the months passed, the venom became more extreme and more personal.

To this day no one can prove exactly what happened that September night just a month before the twins' birthdays. It was a Saturday and the crisp taste of autumn was in the air. The night before the Williams' Family Band played the dance at the community hall. Afterwards, everyone agreed it was their best performance ever and odds were they would win the competition at the state fair next year if they kept playing that way.

It was an undisputed fact that Joe Clinton and his boys arrived in town earlier that afternoon with a delivery from the blacksmith shop for one of the local ranchers.

It was also known that Joe's boys—Zeb, Abe and Hack—didn't try to pick a fight with Jimmy and Chris that day, something that had never happened before.

Later a woman at the bank remembered to have heard someone say he saw the Clinton boys out behind the Williams General Mercantile about sundown, just before closing time, but she couldn't remember who it was and no one ever came forward to verify it. Joe Clinton left town after dropping his boys off to haul his load to his rancher customer.

It was dark, a few minutes past eight o'clock, when the terrifying alarm was raised. "Fire! Fire! Fire at Williams General!" It was a business owner's worst nightmare.

Jimmy and Chris were among the first on the scene and, before any brigade to fight the fire could be organized, rushed in and started hauling as many of the goods out of the store as they could get to. Parker Thompson arrived and began to help. By the time James arrived, the flames had spread and the twins and Parker could no longer save any more merchandise. Apologetically, Jimmy said, "We got as much as we could. It isn't much. It isn't much. We're so sorry. We tried."

James looked at his oldest sons. Their hair was singed from the heat of the fire that took his business. Black soot smudged arms and clothing and their sad, drawn faces. They smelled of smoke. Tears mixed with ash stained their scorched cheeks. They had been first on the scene and had put themselves in danger to save as much as they could and yet were apologizing for not having done more. He could scarcely speak. "Jimmy, Chris, you have worked a miracle here, boys. You've done more than any man could expect."

He paused and placed a loving hand on each of their shoulders. "It's I who owe you an apology. I've been referring to each of you as 'boys.' I won't do it again. You're more men than most of us around here." James pulled them close and whispered. "I love you. Thank God, you're safe."

"James! James! Oh, James, what happened?" It was Sarah who just arrived, weeping and distraught. James turned from his sons to greet her. The twins turned to join the bucket brigade beginning to form, pouring bucket after bucket in an attempt to douse the raging flames.

"Sarah!" They hugged and held each other tightly. Together they numbly watched the fruits of years of labor yield little by little to the consuming blaze.

Then came the cry that made their blood run chill.

"Help! Help me!"

The pitiful wail came from inside the burning building. Without a moment's hesitation, Jimmy and Chris sprang into action and rushed through the open door and out of sight into the sea of flames.

"No!" Sarah screamed, and James held her back from running after them.

The next few moments seemed to pass in surrealistic slow motion for James and Sarah. Anxiously the gathering crowd focused its gaze on the front door. The seconds ticked by into minutes with no sign of the twins. The crackling pyre popped and poked new fingers through the windows on the east side of the building. James glanced over and in the reddish glow saw Zack and Abe Clinton mutely standing and staring. Sarah held her breath while wringing her hands, intently peering at the door. Where were they? Why didn't they come?

Suddenly a shout went up. "Here they come!"

There was a collective cry of relief as the crowd saw the silhouette inside the door. The twins were pushing along a stumbling victim, wet blankets over their heads, and the raspy sound of heavy coughing and choking. Just ten feet more and they would make it. Suddenly, Hack Clinton fell through the door and rolled toward a group of men who rushed forward to pull him away. They began working on him, tearing off charred clothing, bathing him with cool water, bandaging his burns. Nothing serious, fortunately. He would recover.

The attention of the rest of the group remained centered on Chris and Jimmy. One of them fell. The other stooped to help his brother. The thick smoke covered them like a blanket. James and Parker Thompson and two other men rushed into the doorway and carried the twins to safety in their arms.

They were laid gently on the ground. Unmoving. Blackened with soot, their eyes were closed.

"They made it!" Sarah laughed joyfully when she saw them hauled through the door. But as she rushed forward to see them, she knew immediately something was wrong. In an instant Sarah had the perfect knowledge of an anguish so enormous that it consumes every thought and emotion, an agony so deep that it penetrates every nerve and cell.

Sarah's boys were dead.

Later, Mary Thompson would recall that terrible night. "I'll never forget Sarah's wailing for her kids. The heat, the fire crackling. Her crying out. It was like everything came to a standstill except the flickering flame casting its red glow on my best friend huddled pitifully over her motionless twins. It's a scene that will stay with me forever. Even before she reached the boys we knew—we were grieving already."

Sarah wailed. She crouched down, her mind in a fog. Tenderly she lifted lifeless Jimmy close to her bosom, and then Chris. No one moved. She just held them and wept. "Dear Heavenly Father, oh, God! What has happened to my precious boys? They were just children. Why? Why?" Her sobbing cries echoed in a silent heaven.

And then it happened, something so transcendent, so powerful that it swept aside the horror in the twinkling of an eye. A calm began to swell inside of Sarah and with it a wave of peace so comforting and real that it washed over the hot torment like a healing river.

With the flowing comfort came words, whispered over and over in her mind and heart. "Jimmy and Chris are in my hands. They were very brave. They have finished the work I had for them to do. I am so sorry. You must also be brave. You must go on. They are with me."

Right from the start most believed it was arson and most of those who did were willing to point the finger of blame at Zack, Abe and Hack Clinton. Why else were they at the store that night after close of business? Why else was Hack Clinton trapped inside?

They never admitted to it, of course. Folks would shake their heads and say what a shame it was that two of White lake's finest young men should lose their lives saving the likes of one of those worthless Clinton boys.

A real shame.

James and Sarah and the rest of the family chose not to dwell on such things. They mourned deeply. They grieved hard. They hurt bad for a long time.

And they moved on.

That's the way it was done. They knew there was One larger than themselves in charge of all of it and they were content to leave things to Him. It was enough to remember Jimmy and Chris as the heroes they were. For years after the fire, people marveled at the magnificent serenity James and Sarah Williams seemed to possess during the next few days immediately after the tragedy. The community healed because of their strength.

As for Joe Clinton, he never said a thing about that night, but he never again pushed his complaints against James Williams about the land. Later, he paid a visit to apologize and beg James' forgiveness, which was granted with a handshake. Zack, Abe and Hack never said a word. It was like the memory of that night hammered a spike through their tongues. They returned to Mountain View with their father and nevermore set foot in White Lake. It was reported that the four of them moved a few months later back to the Midwest somewhere, but no one knew where for sure.

The twins' funeral was a beautiful thing. It seemed everyone in town and many from across the State came to pay their respects. Most said it wasn't so sad and somber as they expected. It was a good and decent thing to honor two who so courageously gave their lives for another.

In the days that followed, James had a fine display cabinet crafted and hung in the entryway. In a family ceremony, the Williams' placed Jimmy's fiddle and Chris' clarinet inside as a reminder to themselves—not of Jimmy and Chris, for they would never be forgotten—but as a reminder that their lives were not their own.

Shortly after the cabinet was finished, a visitor to the home commented on it. Upon learning what it was, he asked James if the band would ever play again.

James thought it over for a moment. "Play again? Of course we'll play again! Yes, we will play. Only now we will have two angels playing with us."

CB

Monday, September 16.

Today was Edward's next to the last day at Perkins Insurance and Real Estate. Monday he starts a new career at Williams' General Mercantile. I don't know who is the more excited, Edward or me; or even Ben Thompson, for he seems genuinely pleased to have Ed come to work for him. I completely understand his enthusiasm. Ed is so talented and has so much to offer. I love him more every day even though I don't know how that is possible because I love him with my whole being.

I am getting bigger (especially in the middle), so there is more of me for Edward to love! I'm also growing in many other ways. It's like I have been walking around the first twenty years of my life in half darkness, like pre-dawn light. Suddenly the sun has come up and I see things so much more clearly now. Sarah once told me, "If you knew who you were, miracles would happen." I'm starting to see what she means by that.

I fear Sarah will not be with us much longer. I visit every day now. When she has strength to talk, she rarely remembers who I am. Today she thought I was Maggie. "I knew you would come," she said to me. "I got your letter that said you would be here. Would you sing to me?" It was pitiful. I just stroked her hair and sang "Abide With Me," which I know is one of her favorites. She closed her eyes and went to sleep before she could figure out I don't have the beautiful voice her daughter does. Still, some days are better than others. Yesterday she wanted to know if

Ed was playing Jimmy's fiddle that she gave me. She remembered that. I told her "yes."

Ed plays almost every night. He likes Jimmy Williams' fiddle better than his own, but I think he intends to keep them both. It brings me great pleasure to hear him play and brings him joy to do so. He's happier than he has been in several months. I think this decision to change jobs is the best thing that could have happened.

It was something that he agonized over. There were his insurance customers to think about. These past couple of weeks he's been busy visiting them and turning them over to Tom Perkins. He tells me most of them seem supportive, glad for him, and wish him well. One or two don't want to move to Tom, but for the most part that's gone quite smoothly.

The toughest part for him was telling Tom he was pulling out of the Riceland deal to finance the motor inn cabins. It means they won't be built, at least for the time being, unless Tom goes in with Riceland alone, which I don't think he'll do.

It was a decision we talked about, thought about, struggled with and prayed hard about. He felt —we both felt—making the change was the right thing to do, all things considered. So he took a leap of faith.

Our lives have taken one of those forks in the road. It is the sixth secret: Our lives are not our own.

Chapter Eight

Be one.

"I'm disappointed, that's all I can say." Tom Perkins shook his head while Ed cleared the final items from his desk.

There actually wasn't much there that he wanted. It all fit into a shoebox—just a few pictures of Corinne and personal notes. If it weren't for the pictures he'd forgo facing Tom's last shot at persuading him to stay.

"I know, Tom. As I've said before, I'm terribly sorry, but I'm afraid it's something I must do."

When he told Tom of his decision, his old boss had this same "I'm disappointed in you" discussion with him. That was more than four weeks ago. As they went through the transition of shifting all of Ed's customers to him, Tom seemed quite accepting and even supportive of the move. Now that the final day had actually arrived, festering feelings surfaced in an old dialogue.

"How can you simply walk away from the opportunity of a lifetime?"

I'm walking toward one, Ed thought. He shrugged his shoulders. "I haven't come by this decision lightly, Tom. You know that. I know you feel let down about the project, and I'm sorry about that. I truly am. I've given a lot to it and you get the benefit of all that work. It's a great idea and it's not easy to walk away from it like this, but it is for the best. I hope it does well for you."

"Oh, it will," Tom asserted purposefully. "It will make Richard Riceland a lot of money and make me a rich man. It should be a gold mine for you and Corinne, too. You did all the work and you should get the rewards."

"You may be right," Ed nodded ruefully.

"You can change your mind. It's not too late to be wise about this thing."

He paused as if he was considering his friend's counsel, but he remained true to his heart. "Goodbye, Tom. Good luck with the Riceland deal." He shifted the box to his left arm and stuck out his right hand. "Thanks for everything."

Tom firmly and affectionately took the hand in a parting shake. "Okay, Ed. Good luck to you, too."

Then he headed out the door. He was nervous, excited and relieved. He was doing the right thing. Wasn't he?

"Give me a call when you need more insurance!" Tom called as the door shut behind him.

Learning a new business was its own reward. Ben Thompson was true to his word and, from the start, worked closely with his young protégé. The Christmas season was nearly upon them, always the busiest time of the year for the store. The first project placed under Ed's control was the traditional Candy for Kids effort. From its simple beginning when Sarah Williams acted on the noble impulse of her own loving heart, it had grown over the years and decades into a major holiday service movement.

"It's the most significant thing I've ever been involved in, Corinne," he told his wife one night. "It doesn't make us one cent—at least not in any direct way—but I've never felt I've wanted to do anything better than this project. It's the biggest and best thing I've ever done!"

Corinne was sublimely happy with her husband's excitement. This was the Ed she knew—enthused and energetic, focused on something that was meaningful to him.

She noted what a sharp contrast that was to the period when he worked on the Riceland deal for Tom Perkins and the motor inn cabins. No longer did he come home tired and grumpy. No longer did he seem consumed with the intricacies of working the angles for the shrewdest bargain or with accumulating riches in a world gone speculation-crazy. No longer was he frazzled with the stress of providing for his family.

She liked the change. And she was happier, more comfortable, more secure.

"I have ideas," Ed bubbled, "like adding a Christmas parade. It's obviously too late to pull together this year, but everyone I talk to about it thinks it would be a wonderful thing. It would be a big one with floats and bands and decorations, with a visit from Saint Nick, of course. We'd draw entrants from all over the valley and eventually the entire State and region. Think of the visitors that would come to White Lake to be a part of it, to see it!"

"And shop."

"Well, that, too," he grinned.

Ed was a big thinker, with a grandiose idea always churning somewhere inside his head. It was one of the things Corinne loved about her sweetheart. It would, she was convinced, one day make of him a great success. But for now, it was time to reel him in a little bit. "What about Sarah's kids? Her only wish was to quietly make Christmas a little brighter for needy folks in these parts, especially the children."

"That's what's so wonderful and exciting. We lose none of that pure service. It is still the core of the project. So far we have just over a hundred families on the list this year throughout the valley. Mostly farm or ranch families. You know, with the depressed agricultural prices lately, a lot of them are having real trouble hanging on."

"Strange, isn't it?" Corinne mused.

"The families you mean?"

"Yes. I mean with so much prosperity and wealth in this country right now. I mean the economy is better than it's ever been…"

"No kidding. The stock market's like a wild fire. Everyone is getting into it."

"Except us," Corinne reminded.

"Yes, well, with this new job I think soon we'll have a little extra cash. Then we can start putting our money to work for us so we'll have to work less for our money." Ed was a dreamer. "At least we don't have any debt to wrestle with right now."

Corinne was grateful for that. She was very aware how many in the nation and even in White Lake had borrowed heavily—some to get into the climbing stock market—but now they were slaves to the relentless whip of interest payments. She and Ed were united in avoiding that terrible burden, even though it meant sacrificing some things they wanted or needed. Some of her younger friends thought they were foolish not to get in on things while they were going good, and some of them seemed to be making a lot of money, at least on paper. Sometimes it was tempting to follow the crowd and speculate in the market. They resisted, however.

They were plodders when it came to their finances and she preferred it that way. Stay out of debt. Save for a rainy day.

"I think it's sad how the economy seems to be working against folks in farming and ranching right now. I feel bad for those families," Corinne said with heartfelt compassion.

"At least we can help a little with the Candy for Kids project." The spirit of the service began to take on a more personal face for Ed. He knew many of the families on the list. He had been in their homes, pet their dogs, greeted their children. He realized it would be a bleak Christmas this year. Those fathers would have hearts throbbing with pain because they could not provide a little something special for their families at a special season of the year. He became more determined that not one family in the valley would be missed.

"How about Sarah Williams?" Corinne wanted to know.

"Sarah?" Ed asked blankly.

"Is she on your list?"

"Sarah? No, she's not a kid."

"She's very lonely, you know. Seems a shame someone who has given so much should be ignored by the very program she started."

It was a shame and Ed felt it. "I should have thought of that," he admitted with chagrin. "I'll make sure she is honored in a way that she should be. And, of course, we ought to have her over for Christmas dinner and ..."

"I don't know if she can even get out anymore. She's awfully weak now."

Ed was on a roll and scarcely acknowledged his wife's observation. "And come to think of it, there are probably dozens of others like Sarah in White Lake. Old and alone, no family close by any more, good folks whose hands literally built this town!"

Corinne saw that her man had that far away look he got when he was envisioning a new possibility and plan. A big thinker, that Ed Whitmore.

Suddenly his eyes snapped back into focus and locked onto her face. "I've got to get busy. There is a lot more to do on this deal. Dear, you are a genius!"

"I know," Corinne replied modestly.

Tom Perkins' hands trembled uncontrollably in his lap as he sat in Ben Thompson's office. He was in shock, ashen-faced, cold perspiration beaded on his spacious forehead. Ed Whitmore handed him a glass of water, which he took and sipped numbly.

"You heard the news?" Tom asked gravely.

Ben and Ed glanced at each other. "Yes, Tom, we heard," Ben replied. "It came over the radio about twenty minutes ago. They cut right into Perry White's show."

"Unbelievable. It's unbelievable."

Ed was concerned about his friend. "Are you all right, Tom?"

"I just can't believe it," he muttered, wide-eyed.

Ben leaned forward. "Tom, how bad is it? Can you tell?"

He blinked hard. "I don't know yet. Unless there's a miraculous rally, it's pretty bad. I'm pretty much wiped out, I guess."

Like millions in the country, Tom Perkins had invested heavily in the stock market. He had been doing quite well as the economy whistled along, amassing the modest fortune that put him in a position to grow and diversify. It was the foundation upon which he confidently forged ahead with his ambitious motor inn cabins venture. He had routed nearly all his spare cash into stocks. Now the bottom fell out. Today, he was worth less than one tenth what he was just a few days ago.

"I'm sorry, Tom," Ben commiserated. "A lot of us took a big hit."

Tom nodded, somehow comforted by the idea that a great businessman like Ben shared the suffering. Ben would come out okay, he knew, in part because he had not directed so much into the market. Ben's strategy had been to modestly buy land, something he picked up from James and Sarah Williams over the years. Besides, he still ran the mercantile. Ben Thompson would survive this all right. Maybe he could, too.

"Look at this." Ed was staring out Ben's second story office window. Across the street and one block to the east a growing crowd blackened the sidewalk in front of the bank.

"We've got a run," Ben concluded. "I'm guessing Porter Hatch locked his doors over there. If I was bank president, I suppose I would do the same thing. There are a lot of panicked folks right now who don't know what to do. All of us running businesses around here have to keep our heads."

"I can't believe it," Tom kept muttering.

Ed worried about his old boss. He knew how heavily Tom had invested—essentially his entire life's savings. The small amount he set aside for emergencies now sat locked up in White Lake's main bank. No telling when it would open again, if it ever did. Tom's cash flow would be completely cut off, at least for a while.

Ed also realized Tom's insurance business was in great peril. The lure of making lots of money had attracted many small investors, including families like those in White Lake. Like moths to a flame, they had been drawn to the market, pouring all their savings a little at a time into the hottest stocks. When it evaporated practically overnight, many of these good people were devastated financially. They would be forced to cut to the bone just to get by. There would be ripples through the entire economy, like shock waves after a large earthquake. Many of Tom's customers would not be able to pay their premiums and would cancel their policies. New customers would be few and far between. Things were likely going to be very, very tough for a while. Had he not put so much into following the financial fad of stocks speculation, Tom could probably weather the storm and survive. With his losses as great as they seemed to be... well, Ed knew Tom was in for hard times.

Tom left to go to his office, still visibly shaking.

The hours passed into early afternoon. With few customers coming in, Ed had time to think.

As for Corinne and himself, Ed was profoundly relieved and grateful to have escaped the immediate effects. His first sense was one of smugness at his prophetic powers, but his integrity did not allow that thought to take root. The fact was, it was not his genius or prescient capacity that saved them from losing big. If they had any extra cash, he likely would have joined his old boss in the speculation game. Until now, he had not really comprehended the risks. The truth, he told himself, was that his heart and intelligence were no different than anyone else's. He just didn't have the money.

And that brought him to another realization. Many folks who didn't have the money had borrowed heavily. The terms seemed so good and the bet seemed such a sure one. But Ed and Corinne determined debt was a master they would diligently work not to become slaves to.

Ed's love for his wife swelled in that moment. Until now he did not recognize the innate wisdom she possessed. He still didn't understand it, for it worked so differently with him. He studied and plotted and planned and researched and added things up logically. His decisions were based on the facts and, though he was still young, the results bore out the soundness of his judgments. He clearly had a talent for certain business matters. But he had assumed Corinne knew little about such things, although he vaguely acknowledged she tried to stay up by reading at the library. That was an activity he self-centeredly assumed was simply a sweet gesture so she could show interest in his affairs.

That was what she had told him. He felt foolish and ashamed because he realized his air of false superiority had prevented her from really being a full partner in their dealings when it came to their finances. "How stupid of me!" he thought.

Humility and love washed over him as he realized her "pestering" about not going into debt, about his business and about the Riceland deal had saved him from moving too fast. The frustration he felt at the time was replaced by swelling gratitude for her abilities. Without her, he almost certainly would have already rushed into the Riceland deal and the stock market. He could have been ruined. Instead, because of her, he ended up at Williams General on a completely different career path.

No, it wasn't his genius that had saved them—it was hers.

Just how important that was became all the more evident over the next several days and weeks when it was clear the economy would not quickly recover. Reports came in from the East that so deep was the failure of the market that men were leaping out of skyscraper windows in despair to their own deaths.

"Can you imagine that?" Ed asked Ben early one morning before opening the store. They always had a management meeting an hour ahead of unlocking the doors for the day. "How can they do that to their families? It seems to me that's the supreme act of cowardice." He did not mask his disgust.

Ben nodded in agreement. "It is hard to understand, isn't it? Unless you consider that some men are so in love with the power and prestige of wealth, that they are blind to anything else, including their own families, even their own lives."

"It's still a cowardly act."

Ben let it go at that. His young protégé would learn and soften with experience. There were more immediate, local concerns to tackle. "Now, let's figure out a strategy. A lot of White Lake folks are hurting. As far as I can see, it's only going to get worse before it gets better. It means that some who shop with us today won't be able to afford anything in the near future and those who can will buy less. In addition, our suppliers will have a tougher time getting goods to us at a cost we can afford. That all points to declining sales. What do you think we ought to do?"

"I've been thinking about that and agree sales will be down for a while." Before Ed could go on, Tom Perkins, who came bounding breathlessly through the door, suddenly interrupted them.

"Hello, Tom," Ben exclaimed in obvious surprise as he stood up from his chair. "Nice to see you again. What a pleasure…"

"Mrs. Bateman, your secretary, just arrived. I came in behind her." The man seemed distracted, edgy.

"Have a seat, Tom, please."

Tom sat nervously in a padded office chair at the front of Ben's large desk. His hands were clasped tightly, his knuckles white as he unconsciously massaged them vigorously.

"Can we help you, Tom?" Ben's voice was gentle.

Tom Perkins' lip quivered as he fought his emotions. He cleared his throat and shifted awkwardly in his seat, still fidgeting with his hands. The weary, haggard man that sat before them was scarcely recognizable to Ed. This specter had red eyes with dark circles under them, stooped shoulders, tight lips curved down toward a chin stubbled with gray whiskers, a crease of worry etched across his forehead.

This was hardly the same man who, as his boss, appeared confident and assured, a successful businessman with big dreams and significant influence in the community. Now he sat a broken, pitiful soul who had aged a lifetime in just a few weeks. This was a man who had worked hard to get into the economic main stream. He was not, however, prepared for the powerful whirlpool that left him drowning in the wake of the market crash.

"Tom, what's wrong?" Ed tried to sound as gentle as Ben. He truly felt tenderly toward his former mentor.

"Richard Riceland."

"What about him?"

"He's scrambling to cover himself. He is exercising his contract option on all his so-called 'partnerships,' because he's desperate for cash. These small businessmen, if they can't afford to buy out his share, are losing their companies to him. He's crushing the life out of them. He's absolutely ruthless."

"Tom, you didn't sign anything did you?" Ed asked in alarm.

The beaten man acted as if he did not hear the question. "I met a man in Chicago during the summer when I went up there exploring the Riceland deal. You remember that trip, Ed?"

"I remember, Tom."

"Anyway, Riceland's group wanted to make certain I met the gentleman. He was real enthusiastic about his arrangement with Richard Riceland. Best thing since the horseless carriage, according to him. He sure made it sound awfully good."

"Now, that was Augustus Cortland, wasn't it?" Ed recalled Tom mentioning the name that first day back in the office. From that time forward, Tom and Ed had focused on working out a deal with Richard Riceland.

"Huh? Oh, yes, it was. Gus Cortland."

"Cortland Machinery," Ed explained to Ben.

"Oh, yes. Of course, I should have recognized the name. I gather he is the force behind the fastest growing parts manufacturer in the nation."

"That's right," Tom continued. "I spent time with him, heard his 'rags to riches' story and saw his operation. Quite impressive. One of the richest men in Chicago, they say. And he claimed he owed it all to the backing he got from Riceland. It was all very exciting, very persuasive."

"Tom, did you go ahead and sign with Riceland on your own, without me?" Ed's voice quivered, betraying his heightened anxiety.

"No. No, I didn't get that far because of you two. When Ed here decided to leave me and come over to Williams General, Riceland decided he wanted to review the whole deal again. Basically, it meant all the work we did over the past year was down the drain. The deal was dead. I blamed you, Ben, and you, Ed. I despised both of you for it."

"I'm truly sorry you feel that way, Tom," Ben began, "but I …"

"No, please," Tom held up a hand and stopped him. "You don't understand. I'm here to thank you and beg the forgiveness of both of you."

"You what? Whatever for?"

"For saving my life."

"That's a bit dramatic, isn't it, Tom?" Ed quietly interjected. "I'm the one who threw a wrench into the works here. If anyone here is in need of forgiveness, I am."

Tom looked at his talented young friend. He briefly considered what might have been, closed his eyes briefly and shuddered. "I just learned Riceland took control of Cortland Machinery. With the collapse, I guess the company's cash was frozen. An installment to Riceland's group came due and Cortland couldn't make payment. True to his "Raider" moniker, Richard Riceland swept in and seized the enterprise. No extension at all, no compassion. No mercy. Nothing!"

"What does that mean? Did he suspend operations?"

"Stopped the lines dead in their tracks. Not only that, but he's laid off more than half of Cortland's workers, hundreds of men with wives and children to feed."

Edward further observed, "And think of the ripple effect. With Cortland out of production, the factories they supply can't get their parts. They'll have to go into slow down, too, maybe lay off workers themselves."

"This is one of the most sickening things I've heard," Ben exclaimed, shaking his head.

"It seems hard to believe, yet it was all legal, all part of the agreement Gus Cortland signed with Riceland."

"I can believe it," Ed acknowledged. "You know, it was that language in his proposed contract with Tom that me made me mighty uneasy. In fact, that was the main issue we were trying to smooth out this past summer in trying to work out our deal with his group."

"But why would anyone sign something that left the entire company so vulnerable?" Ben wanted to know. His head was shaking even more vigorously.

"It's the lure of easy money to capitalize growth," Tom answered. "That's what it was for me and that's why I didn't want to wait for the bank here to figure out financing of the project. Riceland promised quick and easy growth in a booming economy." He sadly added, "When things are going so good for so long, you don't imagine they could change overnight."

"Hmm. Yes. Well, so you were fortunate that circumstances prevented you from entering into the Riceland agreement. That's no reason to lavish gratitude on Ed and me for 'saving' your life."

"Yes it is. I could have been like Cortland Machinery and a dozen others. The despair would have been too great."

"Despair? Come on, Tom, it's only money."

"It seemed like more than that. You see, this morning, Gus Cortland went to his study, pulled a pistol from his desk drawer and blew his brains out."

ᘓ

"I'm afraid I'm not up to a trim today, dear. Let's wait until the next time. Do you mind?"

Of course I don't mind, Sarah." Corinne returned the nippers to the velvet lining inside the wooden box. She put the box into her handbag and then reached forward and gently pulled the knit warmer more snuggly around the old woman's shoulders.

The fire in the fireplace roared. The room was hot. Corinne wondered if she would have a hard time staying warm enough when she—if she—got to be Sarah's age. The feeling of cold was something she did not easily tolerate. It made her shiver just to think about.

They just sat for several minutes, Sarah napping, and Corinne sitting close by just watching and thinking. How much longer would this amazing woman have? It seemed at times she wanted to be released from the shackles of her fading body to, as she put it, "join my James in glory." At times she straddled the line, one foot in life and one over in the life called death. Other times she had both feet planted firmly in mortality, especially when she thought about her daughter and her family coming to visit. It had been hard on Sarah with all of her children living so far away, so wrapped up in their own lives. It was sobering for Corinne to wonder how she might respond when her own mother became as old.

When Sarah opened her eyes, Corinne noticed the clarity and light in her friend's eyes.

The frail woman smiled brightly. "It's so nice to have you here, dear. You know, Maggie is coming for Thanksgiving this year."

Corinne had heard the promises before. "That's nice. It's not many days away now."

"My hands are cold. Would you mind very much holding them in yours for a little while?"

Corinne shifted from her seat and kneeled beside her friend. "Of course not, Sarah." She tenderly cupped the small, wrinkled hands in her own.

"These are like ice!" She softly pulled their hands to her lips and gently blew, her warm breath kindly caressing the translucent skin.

Sarah shivered and smiled. After several minutes she tipped her head back and sighed. "I miss him terribly, you know."

The old woman weakly pulled her hands back to herself. Corinne let them slip easily from her palms.

"I miss my James. He's been gone for ten years and I still ache. At my age, that's a long time to live hurting."

"I'm sure it must be hard, Sarah."

Perhaps someday you'll have to learn just how hard," she replied. "I hope you do not, child."

Corinne was thoughtful. "Why do we do it? There's so much pain. I mean, early on while you learn to live together, later as you struggle to build a life and raise a family. And then later when you're left alone. If it hurts so much, why do people get married?"

Sarah smiled faintly. "You are wise beyond your years. Thank you, my dear."

Corinne was confused. "Thank me? For what?"

"For reminding a dotty old fool wallowing in a moment of selfish pity that it's all worth it."

"Is it?"

"Yes. Oh, absolutely yes." Sarah brightened as energy visibly flowed into her aged frame. "It takes work, obviously. It takes sacrifice. There are no guarantees beyond the solemn covenant a wife and husband make to each other every single day. But that's the genius of it—the power and promise of marriage is the union of husband and wife for time and all eternity."

"That's our hope, anyway."

"Yes, that is the hope," Sarah repeated. "Yet it is a hope springing from that part of each one of us deep inside that is divine."

"Yes, I know! I feel that sometimes. I know what you are saying about something inside of us being divine. It's like there's a little spark of something greater than just ourselves." Corinne was excited at the connection.

"Marriage between a man and a woman who make a commitment of love to each other, I believe, comes from God. He designed it so that as they unite and become one together, they can realize their highest and holiest aspirations. They can't do it alone; they need each other. It makes men and women complete."

"Is that how it was with you and James?"

"Well, I admit it wasn't much that way at the first. But after all the years we were married, yes, it really was that way."

"So that is why you miss him so much still." Corinne sorted it out in her mind. "Well, of course you miss him! It would be like … like …" She fumbled for an analogy. "Like half of me is gone."

Sarah chuckled at the image. "Yes, his passing ahead certainly left a huge hole. I …" She sighed again.

The old woman's face took on that far away look when someone transcends time and space. Though her eyes were looking in her direction, Corinne saw that Sarah was not seeing her, gazing instead—where? Probably into the past, she decided.

"We worked it out, James and I," she finally said softly. "We made the promise to each other that our home would never be the setting where we aired our differences with each other."

"You never argued or disagreed?" Corinne asked in surprise.

"No. No, of course we disagreed. We had arguments. James certainly wasn't the perfect one of the pair," Sarah quipped, "and even though I was pretty darn close, I still allowed myself a fault once or twice each year."

"But I thought you just said …"

"I said that we never argued at home," Sarah clarified. "Now, we did have some 'strong discussions,' as I recall, in our office up at the store. But, to tell the truth, since we had to walk all the way up there from the house to do it, by the time we got to the store, the anger was usually gone and by then we were too pooped to fight anyway."

"I like that idea," Corinne giggled.

"I know it's fashionable these days for some folks to focus on the differences between men and women. They jest about it and make light of marriage. James and I simply chose to be in love with each other. None of this romantic rubbish of 'falling in' or 'falling out' of love. We just worked at it. And we decided, too, that our home would not be the battleground in any sort of 'war of the sexes,' as they say. We tried to make it a safe place for each other and for our children—a place of order and love and honor and respect for each other."

"I like that!"

"Yes, well these days it sounds terribly old-fashioned, but it worked. James was so good that way. I don't remember any time he ever insulted me or any other woman."

"That's wonderful."

"Of course, I'm a very old woman and my memory is not what it used to be," Sarah winked.

Corinne giggled again.

"But then I choose to have a short memory about certain things. Kind of helps things move along more smoothly when you do, if you know what I mean."

Corinne knew precisely what she meant.

"And, in time, he was equally gracious to me."

Corinne furrowed her brow as she thought of something. "I've heard … I mean I've read that, well, there is a growing voice in certain circles of intellectuals and the 'elite' classes that marriage is a tiresome idea, an institution that was fine in its day but has outlived its usefulness."

"I've heard that, too, dear. That old idea was around decades ago when James and I tied the knot. I suspect it's been around pretty much since Adam and Eve had children. Nothing new under the sun, you know."

"Except that some of these single sophisticates make like they are very happy without it."

"Perhaps," Sarah mused, "but I think it is an incredibly selfish idea that marriage is foolish and children a shame and a burden. I've lived long enough to know that those who pursue it will reap disappointment by and by."

"I don't know," Corinne replied sounding unconvinced. "Maybe it's really not for everyone. It's just that the magazines make single life sound so glamorous."

Sarah squinted her eyes at her young friend and took a deep breath. "Would you mind putting another log on the fire, dear? It's burned down. It seems so cold in here today. Aren't you cold?"

To Corinne, the room was already unbearably warm, but she did as her friend asked. "There we go." The flames happily danced along the length of the dry pine like an eager puppy wagging its tail.

"Oh, thank you. That's better. I wonder why it is so much colder this year. Just one of those years, I guess."

Sarah gazed for a few seconds into the fire. "Corinne, if single life is the most blessed state a person can aspire to, as those magazines seem to imply, why doesn't everyone simply remain single? Would solve a lot of problems, wouldn't it? Why didn't you remain single?"

"Because I want to be a mother and raise a family," Corinne responded reflexively.

"I'm sure you've heard of women who have children without bothering to get married," Sarah reminded.

"Oh, yes!" Corinne quickly replied, "Like Doreen..." She stopped in mid sentence. She did not want to, indeed, she simply could not gossip when in the presence of this wise, great woman.

Sarah continued. "From the dawn of time there have always been those who wade into the stagnant stream of sorrow, my dear. They are lured into impure acts and yield selfishly to the glittering promise of happiness, love and fulfillment. Too late do some realize that instead of lustrous jewels they end up with a handful of counterfeit baubles—pleasure not happiness, lust not love, and emptiness not fulfillment. They sought for joy, but found misery."

"I know all that," Corinne pressed a little impatiently, "but many believe chastity is quite old-fashioned. It's just not as important these days as long as the two people truly love each other." She knew she was just repeating the standard argument gaining popularity with some of her generation. "At least, that's what some well-known people think."

Sarah was indignant. Shaking a bony finger to press her point, she sat forward. "That is a dangerous myth perpetuated by those who want you to join them in their guilt. Don't ever fall for it. Don't let your children fall for it. Chastity brings strength and power to the families and societies and peoples of the earth. That will never change."

Sarah's passion impressed Corinne. She hadn't seen the old woman this lively in many months. "I know you are right, Sarah," she smiled. "I wanted to see how you felt about these ideas coming out. I'm glad you said the things you have about it. It is a matter of respect and... "

"...and love," Sarah finished. "Physical union is a sanctifying, elevating experience within lawful wedlock. But when the fountains of life are neglected the floodgates are opened, pouring out the pollutions of disease, contention, broken homes and broken hearts onto humanity. It poisons and destroys societies, families and individual lives."

"That is one thing I really appreciate about Ed. He's always been gentle and considerate about that part of our relationship."

"That's nice, dear. It sounds like he understands that a woman should be queen of her own body."

"I don't know about that. He just says he loves me and would never—well, you know." Corinne's modesty prevented her from speaking aloud her thought.

Sarah nodded approvingly.

After a while, the fire burned low again. Corinne reluctantly sensed it was time for her to go. Sarah did, too.

"I suppose you'll need to be getting along."

"Yes, I suppose so." She hesitated. "You and James… I mean you were so … so, um, … so united."

"Yes, we were. That's the seventh secret, you know."

"The seventh secret?"

"Yes. The other six are nothing without it."

Corinne strained eagerly. Sarah had spoken of seven secrets that first visit so many months ago. This was the grand key, the final mystery to happiness in marriage and life.

"Be one."

Corinne listened for more, but Sarah simply repeated it. "Be one."

Corinne let that soak in, like cool water on parched land. Yes, she understood. "I yearn for that with Ed."

Sarah took measure of her young friend. "You have a good start," she pronounced at length, "a very good start."

"Oh, I hope so. Do you really think so?"

"Yes, of course you do, dear." Sarah sat up in her chair and reached forward. Corinne took her left hand. Sarah then placed her right hand on top. They sat for a few moments like that, Sarah just holding Corinne's hand in both of hers. Finally, she spoke again.

"James and I had three little rules that helped us be as one. I think I can entrust them to you. Do you mind?"

Corinne suddenly felt as if she was granted a great and special honor. She leaned closer and eagerly nodded. "Please. I would love to know. What are the three rules?"

"They are very simple; just common sense, really." Sarah realized her young friend might have overestimated what she was about to share. They were just little things James and she had decided together over the years, not the three secrets of life. Or were they?

"First, promise each other never to wrestle words with each other, not even in jest. Never cut or criticize, even the name of 'teasing' or 'having fun.' Just avoid that temptation while you are in each other's presence and, of course, neither of you would even harbor a thought of being disloyal in your speaking to others when apart. Many make a great joke of their marriages and spouses. As the saying goes, 'Teasing in jest becomes earnest by practice'."

"We can do that," Corinne asserted. "We already do that. Respect each other, really."

"Second, solemnly promise never to keep a secret from each other, no matter what. You have to be completely transparent to each other's view. Your soul must continually be as clear as crystal to him and you must be able to see each moment directly into his heart."

"I think we can do that, with a little work," Corinne responded. Ed *could* be withdrawn, at times, she secretly thought.

"Of course you can, dear. The third thing…"

Corrine eyes brightened as she eagerly listened.

The third thing is to remember that your home belongs only to you, your husband and God. While you keep no secrets from each other, you must jealously guard the privacy of what goes on in your marriage, your heart and your home. Others on the outside, even your close family—well it's just none of their business."

Corrine nodded.

"Naturally, you'll have struggles and difficulty from time to time," Sarah continued as she sat back in her chair. "Don't go running off crying to your mother or anyone else," she said with a wry smile at the corners of her mouth. "Preserve and protect your private lives from mother and father, brother and sister, and from all the world. You two, with God's help, you build your own quiet world."

Corinne reflected silently. At length she said softly, "I think I see. The three rules make sense. I'm going to try. And I believe Ed will want to try, too. I know now our marriage cannot be like yours and James. It should not be. It must be our own and we can make it as sweet and as glorious as we choose. Thank you, Sarah. Thank you from the bottom of my heart."

Corinne leaned forward a little more and kissed her old friend gently on the forehead. Sarah let go of her hand, reached up and patted her on the cheek.

Corinne stood to leave. "Next time, I'll trim those nails of yours."

"Yes. Next time."

Ↄ

The band played on.

Of course, it was never the same after Jimmy and Chris died. James and Sarah persisted for the benefit of their children, or so they told themselves. In more reflective moments they both realized there was something healing about keeping the band going. Besides, their music was still in demand throughout the community. Yet it was only natural that a piece of their enthusiasm and joy had flown with their sons when they perished saving the Clinton boys.

Still, they played on.

The twins had been the spark and vinegar of the group. Their blend of energy and talent was the perfect recipe for popularity. The other children understood that instinctively. Not that Frank and Peter and Merlin didn't play well. They were very talented, too. But everyone knew they didn't have the same special gift that their older brothers had. The three accepted that and it never worried them much. They just did their best, had fun, and kept it going as long as folks in White Lake still wanted to hear them play.

So they played on.

With Maggie it was different. She possessed extraordinary ability, even beyond that of the twins, and in time she took their place as the crowd favorite wherever the Williams Family Band performed. They said she sang with the voice of an angel. She took lessons and worked hard to develop her natural God-given gift. She went on to win many competitions and even made a record album, which sold well in the region.

As Maggie's success grew, the importance of the band to the family faded. Their last performance came at the Fall Festival near the 10th anniversary of the fire. As they played, James looked out on the happily dancing White Lake crowd. He was struck at how many there knew nothing about that day—children who were not yet born or too young to remember, and a large number of families who had moved to White Lake since that fateful day. Though still a big part of its history, the tragic event was not as important to the rapidly growing community as it once was. Time passed; healing happened. The page of history turned.

It would always loom large in the lives of Sarah and James, of course. Time would never fully erase the pain of that terrible loss.

What the townsfolk couldn't see was that in the days and weeks after the fire the Williams family was numbed into a grief that made every action painful. Everything took the greatest effort. Fixing the meals hurt. Preparing for the funeral hurt. Explaining things to their mournful small children hurt. Tidying the house, doing the laundry, feeding the livestock, handling the shopping, awaking each morning and getting dressed—everything hurt.

"I can't do it," Sarah told James on the day after the funeral.

James had no strength of his own. Where would he find any to lend his wife in her time of need? The loss for both of them was seemingly unbearable. His sons were no more. How could they go on? And the store ruined—the mere thought of cleaning up and rebuilding was thoroughly exhausting. Every muscle and joint ached with the pain of profound sadness. Yet his wife needed him to be strong.

"Come here." Tenderly he held Sarah in his arms. She felt safe in his embrace, comforted in his loving gesture. But her pain did not leave. She began sobbing softly and he felt a lump come to his own throat as tears stung his eyes. "It will take time," he whispered. "Let's give it some time."

For the next several weeks that was how they endured—he holding her, she holding him, both of them holding their heartbroken children and all saying, "Let's give it some time."

Giving it time meant getting away for a little while. After the funeral they all traveled down to Marshville where they had family on both sides. They stayed with Sarah's sister Emily. It was a time for healing and so it was time to be cradled in the larger family circle. The children needed it. Sarah needed it.

They stayed for the rest of that month and into the second week of the next. James made occasional visits to their Marshville store, but his heart and mind were not in it. He still hurt.

He knew, however, that hurt or no, when Sarah was strong enough, he'd have to leave her and the children in Marshville and head home back to White Lake to rebuild the store in the aftermath of the fire. His business could not be neglected much longer, especially with the busy Christmas season practically upon them.

Finally the day arrived that James halfheartedly made the long trip back to White Lake. He could delay taking care of business no longer. He arrived at the house late at night, finding things just as they had left them. He built a comfortable fire in the fireplace, prepared his night clothes and went to bed dreading the next morning when he would make the lonely walk to the site where his and Sarah's store once stood and where their sons had perished.

The air was cold and crisp that morning. The sun shone brightly, though devoid of comforting warmth. James stepped from the front door onto the porch and could feel the exposed skin on his face tighten on his cheekbones. His breath hung on his mouth and nose like reluctant clouds. The blood drained from the tips of his ears. He pulled his hat deeper onto his head, tightened the woolen scarf draped about his neck and stepped quickly down the steps onto the sidewalk.

The bustle of folks seemed unusual for a morning like this.

Across the street he could see Jack Dayton, the postman, making a delivery.

"Nice to see you back, James!" Jack called and waved. "Sorry about the fire."

James forced a smile and a wave back. "Thanks, Jack," he weakly replied. Maybe he'd come back too soon after all.

He turned north on Washington Avenue, three blocks to go. Forrest Martin, a farmer who had been a regular customer, was in his wagon headed south pulled by his team. He waved too.

"Tough luck, James."

James nodded, "Thanks, Forrest." He was glad Forrest was not the talkative type and that he drove on. He found it difficult to even greet his old friends, let alone talk about something that was so raw and sensitive as burying his sons.

As he approached the intersection of Washington and Main, Sheriff Jensen stepped out of his office and waved to James from his doorway.

"Glad to have you back, James. We're ready for you."

James knew the community must be ready for him to get his store back in order. They relied on him. And it wouldn't be long before the Senate would be back in session and he would have to attend to that, as well. It was his sense of duty that pulled him away from his family even as they all mended emotionally from the loss. He wished he could say it was nice to be back. It was too soon. The pain would take more time to heal. But he had to forge ahead. "Thank you, Niles."

He turned west on Main Street. Only one block to the store, but he was suddenly confused. Where were the ruins from the fire? Instead of charred rubble, he saw a freshly painted storefront and a new sign "Williams General Mercantile." As he approached, Parker Thompson came out and greeted him with a big broad smile and a vigorous handshake.

"Welcome back, James!"

James was astounded. He turned and became aware that the street was filling with well-wishers. They emerged from the shops, from their carriages, from the bank, and from the diner. They seemed to appear from everywhere. All of them were smiling and waving.

"I ... I don't understand ... I ..."

"Here." Parker took him by the arm. "Take a look inside."

Everything was perfect. New displays, new counter, a restored cash register, and freshly stocked with every item they had ever carried. It smelled fresh, inviting. Even Sarah's candy kitchen gleamed with new pots and pans and utensils from the northwest corner of the store. Everything was ready for the important Christmas season.

James was absolutely stunned. Now he knew what Niles meant when he said "We're ready for you." While he was helping his family in Marshville, under the direction of Parker Thompson, White Lake had completely rebuilt his store. Lumber was donated. The bank financed at no charge the purchase of paint and counters and glass and other materials and goods. Suppliers donated what merchandise they could and offered at their cost anything else needed. Women, men and children from throughout the entire valley came willingly to help clean up and fix up.

James turned to Parker who led him back through the door where the smiling crowd greeted him with cheers and applause. Parker handed him new keys to the front door saying, "This is a gift from all of us to you. After everything you and Sarah have done for White Lake, it is the least we can do."

James numbly grasped the string of keys. He looked at Parker. He looked at the store. He turned to the crowd. "I ... I don't know what to say. I ... well, thank you. Thank you, every one."

Then this man who had made himself be so strong when he buried his sons, who had shouldered the burden of caring for a grieving wife and four small children, who had dutifully pushed his aching bones back home to begin the hard labor of rebuilding— this man who had maintained control of his emotions through it all was now overcome. The floodgates of feelings were unlocked. James sat down on the doorway step, put his face in his hands and for the first time since his sons died, James loudly and openly cried.

The days turned into months and the months into years for James and Sarah. Frank was the first in the family to ever go to college. They were proud that day when they put him on the train headed east, suitcases in hand and big dreams in his heart. He studied medicine in Pennsylvania. He met a beautiful young woman whom he invited to become his wife, and they remained in the Philadelphia area where they raised two daughters and where Frank had a successful family practice. They visited White Lake for two weeks every summer until the girls were grown. Frank unexpectedly died not long afterward and his wife, Phyllis, about two years later in an automobile accident.

Peter, on the other hand, headed west to the coast in sunny southern California. Business was his game and he made his living selling fruit. It wasn't the side of the road or farmer's market type fruit selling that he did. He arranged large deals with huge companies throughout the United States and overseas. He traveled abroad often and James and Sarah received cards from him from exotic places like Hong Kong and New Zealand and South America. He married once upon a time, but his wife left him for another man six years later. When they divorced, they had no children, and he had never married again.

Merlin was the brain in the family. He finished high school a year early and won an award to attend Harvard in Boston. He obtained a law degree, married Sheryl and set up a very successful practice in Boston. James and Sarah didn't get to see them or the grandkids much, but one year they did take the train back east and spent a wonderful time with the family touring some of the nation's historical sites.

Then there was Maggie, the jewel of the valley. Like her older brother Peter, she, too, made her way west to California. Things were happening there and they wanted talented people to be in moving pictures. She appeared in some, sang a bit, and met Paul Smith with whom she fell madly in love. They married and Maggie almost immediately became pregnant with their first child. Paul was a lawyer and worked for one of the largest banks on the west coast, so Maggie devoted her considerable talent and energy to being a mother. They had six children.

They visited James and Sarah two or three times during the year. As the grandchildren grew and had children of their own and as Maggie and Paul became older themselves, the visits became less frequent. Still, after her father died, Maggie wrote to her mother often. In this last letter it said she felt it was time to come visit White Lake again. Maybe at Thanksgiving or Christmas.

Meanwhile, Sarah's candies became so popular they had to build a small factory to keep up with the demand. They put it up on some acreage they owned just north of town. At its Christmas peak, they recruited more than fifty folks from the valley to work for them. They began packaging and shipping all over the United States and into Canada. Then, because of Peter's connections, they even shipped some overseas. Those were busy and exciting times. As the business grew, their factory became too small to keep up with demand and they faced a crossroads. They could go into debt to finance expanding their capacity or they could sell.

A large conglomerate from Minneapolis made an offer to buy Williams Enterprises. James and Sarah were not interested in selling their store, which was also doing well, but wanted to know if the group might be interested in buying the candy operations alone. For Sarah, it meant letting go of something she had nurtured from its infancy into a booming success, and that would be hard.

In the end, however, the freedom from the day-to-day worries involved was more appealing at that stage in their lives than hanging on to the candy manufacturing business. They sold it for a very nice sum, but more importantly negotiated the creation of a foundation so that Sarah's concern for poor children at Christmas could expand nationwide. Children who otherwise would not experience the joys of the season would receive presents— including candy that still bore her name. While different establishments sponsored the cause throughout the country, in White Lake and surrounding regions, Williams General continued to anchor that warm tradition every year.

James never did retire. He gradually gave up management of daily operations to William Thompson, Parker's son and Ben Thompson's father. But he retained a leadership role and would usually go into the office once a week or so well into his seventies, right up to the time he died.

In the meantime, he and Sarah spent more time involved in other philanthropic activities, their source of vitality in their later years. Sarah would joke that the reason they stayed so busy with volunteer work was that they were like old pumps at the well. "If we sat around unused too long we'd just get rusty. You gotta' keep pumping 'til the well runs dry."

The well ran dry for James first. His passing was peaceful, but left Sarah mourning once again for loss of one she loved. Over the years the pain subsided, but the loneliness never did.

Now Sarah rocked back and forth in her rocking chair. She was by herself again. Corinne was gone—she had left about twenty minutes before, she figured.

Then the old woman remembered something. She reached for the pencil and pad of paper she kept on the lamp stand beside her overstuffed rocker. She scribbled a quick note, folded the paper in half and shakily scrawled a name across the blank space.

She went back to rocking. The hour grew late and it was getting cold. The fire had died down to a few glowing embers, interspersed with an occasional burst of bluish flame spitting upward in a vain attempt to recapture its former blaze of glory.

Life was something like that, Sarah mused. You blaze away in youthful glory, changing to a steady, warming heat, finally dying to glowing embers and then…

"I'm so lonely!" Sarah spoke out loud, though she knew no one would hear her voice. So what if they did. She didn't care. She was an old woman now and could say what she wanted when she wanted. The well was nearly dry; the fire was just a few embers glowing from a pile of ashes.

It was twelve years ago now. "You left me alone, James. I miss you so." Sarah reached for the poker to try and stir up a little more heat but it slipped from her frail grasp. She didn't have the energy to get up and retrieve it, so she sat back and closed her eyes.

The cold crept in like a circling pack of wolves.

"James, I have a new friend. Corinne is her name. She is a real jewel. 'The jewel of the valley.'" Sarah giggled softly. "Her husband is Edward. Ed Whitmore. You'd like him, James, a young man cut out of the same cloth as you. Ben Thompson—you know, Billy's boy—Ben's minding the store now. Anyway, as I was saying, Ben got Edward on board over at the store, which was a good job. He's handling the Christmas candy project this year. You'd like him all right. Reminds me of you in a lot of ways. And Corinne is so much like I was at her age."

Sarah drew her wrap tighter around her neck and shoulders. She closed her eyes again.

"I miss you, James," she said again. "You left me alone. It's like I'm left with only one hand. It's like you always used to say, 'One hand cannot applaud alone'." It was so cold and Sarah stopped rocking.

She remained motionless, eyes closed and dozed for she didn't know how long. She figured it must have been a good while, for when she awoke the room was considerably brighter and warmer. A lively fire danced cheerfully in the hearth.

"There now, isn't that just about how you like it?"

Sarah heard the voice, but could not immediately see her benefactor. "Yes. Thank you. It's perfect." It felt cozy and comfortable, right down deep in her bones.

"Well then, I think it's about time you got up out of that chair and said Hello!"

Sarah now recognized the voice coming from behind her. "James!" She leaped up and whirled around.

James laughed, that sparkling, bubbling stream kind of laughter that melted her from the first time they met. "Well now, aren't you a sight for sore eyes."

"James Williams, I can't believe it's really you! How on earth did you get here? And just look at you. Now don't go letting that head of yours be getting too big about it, but you look marvelous for a man your age!"

"Ah, my queen, you ought to see yourself. What a beauty you are! The picture of perfection."

"James, you always did flatter me with that silver tongue of yours. And you know how I love it so," Sarah grinned. She was comfortable and confused, excited, happy and curious all at once. She hadn't felt this good, this alive, in years. "What in heaven's name are you doing here?"

195

"I'm so glad you mentioned that. As a matter of fact, I'm here in heaven's name for you!"

"This is so exciting!" Sarah bubbled. She felt strong, energized, like that teenager almost seventy years ago meeting that dreamboat James Williams for the first time at the Marshville barn dance.

"Come on, dear," James said, taking his bride by the hand. "Are you ready?"

Sarah looked around her home one last time. So many memories. So much of love and life. Her gaze rested upon the frail frame of an old woman slumped in the overstuffed chair. There was a smile on her face.

"Okay," she said. "I'm ready."

"Let's go home."

○ℬ

Wednesday, November 13.

Sarah Williams passed away last night. Ben Thompson found her this morning when he went to call on her. They figure it was probably just a few hours after I visited with her. They said it must have been real peaceful, because she was sleeping. Ben told me and Edward that it didn't seem at first like she was gone because there was this glow about her. She was radiant even in death. The funeral is set for this coming Saturday to give time for her family to come in.

Maggie called on the telephone. She said Ben gave her my number when he telephoned with the sorrowful news. She told me she was planning to be out there in a few weeks, did I know that? I didn't know why she wanted to tell me that, except maybe she was feeling a little guilty about not being here before her mother died. I just said yes, I knew that. Her mother talked about the letter a lot and was real happy that you were planning to come. That seemed to make Maggie feel a little better.

She told me how grateful she was to me that I looked after her mother these past few months. I told her that I'm the one who should be grateful. But I don't think Maggie understood. She's planning on being here in White Lake for the funeral and thinks Peter is, too. She hadn't talked to Merlin yet, but expects he will make it out as well. She didn't know about all the grandkids, but hoped most of them would come.

I didn't do her feet that last visit. "Next time," Sarah said.

I wonder if they will trim her nails before the funeral.

Chapter Nine

Now an old woman herself, Corinne Whitmore turned the last leaf of the old leather journal and sighed. Those were days never to be forgotten. Sarah Williams had been a mentor that first year of her marriage.

No, Corinne decided, she was more than that. She was a mother and grandmother and friend, an accomplished and remarkable woman who had traveled ahead on life's journey and who was eager to share the wisdom of her adventure with a young, naïve bride.

She ran her fingers gently over the pebbly grain of the front cover. The embossed gold lettering, once spelling out "Journal", was peeled and faded, barely decipherable. It contained only that first year of their marriage, up to Sarah's death. After the funeral, Corinne started a new volume. It just seemed right. The birth of Edward, Jr. just a few short weeks later opened a new chapter in her life and so she started keeping her thoughts in a separate record.

She was a faithful journal-keeper all her adult life. "Don't know if they'll do anybody any good," she thought, "but maybe someone in the family will find an entry or two a little interesting or useful." She opened the little volume held in her hands again. It smelled old—kind of musty, mixed with the aroma of ancient leather.

Edward was never much of a journal writer. When he passed on nine years earlier, Corinne went through his things and found a few staggered attempts at different times over the years, but for some reason he never stayed with it long.

His life was recorded in the hearts and memories of those whom he served.

He loved his work at Williams General. When he retired, he was serving as its president and had watched it evolve from a progressive regional general merchandise outlet into a major department store with significant presence throughout the western half of the United States. They reorganized and incorporated as WTW, Inc., for Williams, Thompson and Whitmore. They retained the Williams brand name, the famous JS Williams' stores. "JS" was in honor of James and Sarah. As the mall concept became popular, JS Williams' were often one of the large department stores invited to anchor.

They still sold Sarah's candies, although it was made in staggering quantities by the company in Minneapolis which bought it decades ago. That purchase had proved very profitable for them.

Edward was a truly capable businessman and provided well for his family. "Not really rich, like Rockefeller rich," Corinne would say, "but sufficient for our needs plus a few of the good things in life."

With seven children and economic uncertainties, that was an accomplishment.

"He could have been rich," Corinne thought. "These youngsters today, men and women both just get consumed with making the almighty dollar. Why if they spent even a tenth of the time working on their families as they do on making their money, this world would be a whole lot better off."

She loved Edward's perspective on those kinds of things. She and the family came first to him. He didn't say it, didn't write it anywhere. He didn't have to. He just had his priorities and everyone knew it. Corinne remembered talking to him about it one quiet evening after dinner when he had been president of WTW for a few years.

"Do you know what your business is?" she had once asked reflectively.

"Yes, I do," he replied, "but what do you think it is?"

"Well, it's for sure not clothing or appliances or shoes, and such."

"That's what I sell."

"I know. But you know what I mean."

He chuckled. "You're right. I do know."

His business, they concluded, was people. His service was his life. His values were such that God came first and then Corinne and the kids and, in later years, the grandchildren. His best service was always devoted there.

He also felt a proud duty to his community and nation. And though he never served in any elective office like James Williams had, he was forthright in expressing his ideas and using his influence for good about those issues that affected personal freedoms and that he believed would help make White Lake a better place. His business was just an extension of his spirit of service. The tradition started with the vision of the founders, James and Sarah. It continued with the Thompsons, Parker, William and Ben. Edward understood it, loved it and expanded it.

His service was his life. "And it was a good life," Corinne recalled.

Children who otherwise would have nothing found gifts of shoes, clothing and toys, along with Sarah's candy each Christmas. They—and often their parents—never knew who was behind it all.

Men trying to feed their families who could not otherwise find work were given chances to earn a few dollars on the loading dock or stocking shelves at night or counting inventory. Other employees could have performed these temporary jobs, but the work was shared with those who needed to work. Dignity was restored and hope renewed. And as with the candy tradition, many never understood or knew who made it possible.

When ball fields were built for the youth, Edward was there, a shovel in one hand and a rake in the other.

Ed Whitmore was there when bonds had to be sold for the war. He was still there afterward to help White Lake mourn its dead youth, a costly contribution to the cause.

He was there, quietly behind the scenes, to help the community grow and mature, including the first motor inn cabins. He smiled and had to swallow hard on that one, thinking (however briefly) of what "might have been."

He was there when the first family of African descent moved into White Lake. Jeff Cooper came from Mississippi with his wife and three young daughters. They were just looking for a better life. A few gave a cold response to these good folk because they were a little different. "I guess they didn't know how to act around them," Corinne concluded, "because they were the first of their skin color to move into the valley." Edward found Jeff a job over at the bakery and she and Ed invited them over for dinner and helped them get moved into a small place up in the northeast part of town.

In a short time, nobody in town thought anything about the Coopers being "different." They were just White Lake folks like everyone else around. When they moved a few years later out to the Los Angeles area, Corinne and Ed were truly sad to see them leave.

Ed found pleasure in playing his fiddle. "We should have had a family band," Corinne thought. "He was good," although she knew he would have totally balked at the idea of actually playing his music in front of someone other than his own family.

He wrote a few songs that the family pulled out at special occasions like Thanksgiving and Christmas. They'd sing them together at these events, everyone would say what good songs they were and that Ed should get them published. He would say what a good job they did in singing them and yes, maybe they should go record them somewhere. They could put them in the JS Williams' stores, he'd say. He'd buy one for each of them so, with grandkids and everyone, they could sell 25 records. Everyone would laugh heartily, even though it was the same joke every time.

Then they'd put the music away for another year.

"Ed Whitmore," Corinne spoke out loud, "you were a decent, honest man."

She looked at the small journal in her lap again. She once expressed the hope there that she might have a marriage like James' and Sarah's. "*That* never happened!" Corinne chuckled. Sarah and James had the perfect marriage, or so she thought. Her marriage to Edward had been so… well, so normal. Wonderful, deep, good—but pretty normal when all was said and done.

Or was it? "I wonder what Sarah would say about me and Ed if she were here," Corinne pondered with a sigh. "She'd probably have a totally different view than I do."

Corinne flipped another page and glanced at her writing there.

"Love not shared is no love at all…"

Corinne thought of toenails and her first bumbling attempts to use the nail nippers Sarah had given to Ed and her. Funny, she thought, that it would come to mind after all these years. She flipped through more pages.

"Forgive, let it go, leave it alone…"

"Remember who you are, and miracles will happen…"

Sarah and James. The perfect couple, the perfect marriage, Corinne smiled. How young and naïve she had been. How wise and knowing Sarah seemed back then. Corinne realized now, of course, that Sarah and James had as many struggles and worked as hard at things as any couple. Her wisdom was a simple kind, borne of long experience. It was only after long years of experience with Ed that Corinne really understood.

"You can't be home until you are home..."

Corinne remembered how good Ed was with the kids. Home was definitely where he liked to be. It was where she liked to be when he was there.

"If you miss the joy, you miss it all..."

Corinne smiled as she read that. Life with Ed, all in all, truly had been a joy. Pangs of loneliness crept in with the memory. She missed him.

"Our lives are not our own..."

"Be one..."

Yes, she decided, it had been a good marriage. She and Edward were good together. It was a good life. Now it seemed so very empty without him. Oh, she believed she would be with him again one day, and that was her hope. They had made sacred vows before God to seal their love beyond the "until death do we part" usual divorce clause. But even with that faith, she sometimes got terribly lonely.

She didn't let herself reflect on it too long. That wedding was coming up for their great granddaughter. "Ed." Corinne sometimes spoke to him as if he was present. "Are you thinking what I'm thinking?" She was sure he was. Or, at least, would be if he were there.

Corinne placed her reading glasses on the small table by her chair and closed the old journal. She already picked out what she would wear to the wedding and reception for Michelle and Mark tomorrow. She earlier settled on the dark blue dress with the embedded leaf print. Her black heels would go with that and, she decided, no hat.

She still needed to find that gift for the newlywed couple. Only now she had a good idea. When she returned to the attic, she would look for a certain small wooden box. She chuckled out loud. She could picture the look on the young couple's face when they opened it. It would be the perfect gift.

As she stood, a loose, folded paper fluttered from the pages of the book and drifted to the hardwood floor.

"What's this?" Corinne muttered, a little annoyed at the clutter.

"To: Corinne Whitmore"

It was Sarah's handwriting.

"I don't remember seeing this before," Sarah thought. With stiff fingers she retrieved it from its resting place. She fumbled to find her glasses again. "Can't see to read a thing without them," she complained. Carefully she unfolded the yellowed note.

It was the one Sarah wrote to her after Corinne left the day that Sarah passed on. Corinne sat down. She *had* forgotten all about it, but now it spoke to her with a timeliness that seemed at once eerie and miraculous.

"Love flies on the wings of forever."

ଓଃ

Epilogue

Michelle Jensen laughed gleefully. She sat cross-legged on the carpeted floor of a sparsely decorated apartment on the outskirts of White Lake. Her bare feet protruded from a comfortable pair of faded blue jeans.

"Look! More towels!" She crumpled up the wrapping paper and tossed it into a large paper sack obtained from the local grocery store.

"Okay," her new husband Mark replied. "So now we have, like five hundred towels for each room of the house. We ought to be the cleanest couple around."

Michelle giggled appreciatively at her husband's wit. "So, who sent that set?" She grabbed her little register to log an entry. This would make up her list when later she would write notes on her "Thank You" cards.

"Umm, looks like the Petersons."

"Which ones?"

"Oh. Uh, Gerald and Sharon. You know, the guy with the bald head, thick black glasses."

"Oh, yes. She teaches aerobics at the rec center. They have three little girls. Well, how sweet." Michelle held up one of the hand towels so they both could admire it.

Mark was unimpressed. "What's next?"

"How about this one?"

"Cool." He took a cubical package from his wife's hand. It was his turn to open a present. "Thank you, Mrs. Jensen."

Michelle smiled. "Mrs. Jensen," she repeated. She said it once more, like a shopper trying on a new dress. "Mrs. Jensen. I like the sound of that, don't you?"

"You bet I do!" he replied enthusiastically. "Hey, look at this! A new toaster! Did we get any toasters yet?"

"Only one. And who brought this one?"

"It says, 'From Stephanie Berge'. Do you know her?"

"Yes. A friend from college. A single girl who is worried she'll never get married. It's like she's totally worried about it all the time. We had Psych class together."

"That's cool. Hey here's one. Your turn." He handed a small rectangular gift to Michelle.

"Hey, this one's from Grammo. Awesome!" Michelle tore eagerly at the wrapping. It gave way to reveal a wooden box with a golden clasp at the front. Carefully she unlocked the clasp and lifted the hinged top.

"What is it?"

"I... I'm not sure. Here, let's see what the card says."

Mark was puzzled. "Whoa! It's like a pair of funky-looking scissors." He reached in and removed the implement from its worn velvet space. "What is this thing?"

Michelle meanwhile opened the envelope containing the card. She read it silently then looked at Mark. She says ... well, let me just read it to you."

Dear Mark and Michelle,

Congratulations on your marriage. This pair of nail nippers was the best gift I could think of to give you as you start your life together. Come over and visit me soon. And bring the nippers with you.

Love, Grammo

"What the heck are 'nail nippers'?" Mark wanted to know.

Michelle held them up for closer inspection. "I don't know. I guess you use them to cut your nails, you know, like toe nails and finger nails, or something."

"Oh, gross! Why did she send us something like that? I mean, they're not even new! She's so old. Maybe she's like, you know, senile or something."

When Mark finished his little reactive speech, he looked up from the nippers into Michelle's face. He shriveled beneath the intensity of The Look. He knew he had done something wrong, but hadn't quite put it together yet. He didn't know what to do or say.

"Hey, at least it's the first one we got," he meekly offered.

She tried to hold it, but it was no use. The Look melted from Michelle's face as she erupted into laughter. "Okay. I admit it's a bit strange, but she is one of the sweetest old ladies in the world. It's like she and her husband had this super fantastic marriage, kind of legendary. She is totally awesome."

"Well, anyone who is totally awesome to my bride is someone I definitely have to get to know better. Why don't we go over next Sunday after church? We don't have anything going on then, do we?"

"That would be super. I'll let her know." Michelle set the little box aside, making a mental note to be sure and take it with her next Sunday.

"What's next?"

The Wedding Gift

ABOUT THE AUTHOR

Jesse L. Dunn is a business executive and author. He started "real life" as a teacher and imagines in his heart that teaching is still the most enjoyable service he has to offer in this world.

He is author of *TACT: The Roots of Legendary Service, The Man Who Would Be Added Upon* (both available at amazon.com), and penned a trilogy under the name "Jess Lamont" that includes *Peter's Garden* (available at amazon.com), *Peter's Quest*, and *Peter's Glory*, which are in preparation for upcoming publication.

www.ingramcontent.com/pod-product-compliance
Lightning Source LLC
Chambersburg PA
CBHW051821020726
47502CB00005B/1565